THE NIGHT THE DOORBELL RANG

CHALON J. HARRIS

For Atice L. Harris: 1973-2005

Part I: Cheryl

1

I REMEMBER THE DOORBELL RINGING. I thought I was dreaming still, but when it rang a second time, it startled me awake. I opened my eyes and the bedroom was dark. Hazy silhouettes of the dresser and nightstand came into view. Glancing toward the window, even with the curtains drawn I could tell there was no sign of the sun rising anytime soon. I turned to the bedside clock and checked the time. The brightness made my eyes hurt, and the well-lit numbers were a blur.

2:17 a.m. Who the hell was ringing the bell at almost 2:30 in the morning? I looked over at Jerry — Gerald, when I was upset with him — who was still sound asleep. He let out that rumbling snore, the one that always came after a few evening beers.

They must have had the wrong house, and I had no interest in getting up. I rolled over and pulled the blankets back over me. Just as I begin to doze off, the bell rang a third time, quickly followed by a fourth. "Jerry, wake up." I grabbed hold of his arm and shook him.

"What time is it, Cheryl? It's not even daylight yet. Are you okay, honey?"

The doorbell rang again and snapped me out of my sleepy fog. "Jerry, it's almost 2:30 and someone is ringing the doorbell."

"Probably some kids playing a prank," he said before rolling over away from me and pulling the covers up to his neck.

Jerry hated being woken up. He said it stemmed from his time as a young man in the Navy when he'd be woken up throughout the night for emergency training drills, followed by his twenty-six years as a police officer at the Boston Police Department. Thirteen of those years had been spent as a homicide detective, where he would receive phone calls at all hours—"callouts," as the guys on the force had called them. It seemed most of the murders those days took place in the middle of the night. Even though his title was Homicide Detective, he and his team worked on all the violent crimes in Boston's West End area.

He'd resigned from the force two years ago, at age fifty-four. Jerry loved his job and could have worked well into his sixties, but after the gruesome and very publicized murder of fourteen-year-old Jenny Wilson went cold, he had never been able to forgive himself.

And even though Jerry's career had exposed him to the worst in people, he wasn't callused by it. I loved that about him. We both believed that overall, people are good. Some just choose the wrong path or are products of their environment. But that doesn't account for most people. I think that's why Jerry was able to remain so kind and selfless.

"It has rung four times now. Kids playing pranks don't stay on the porch and keep ringing. Honey, I'm worried."

Jerry and I lived in a modest suburban home in the suburbs of Nashua, New Hampshire, about thirty-five miles outside of Boston. Our house sat in the quiet neighborhood of Riverbend Gated Community, which never had too many strangers passing through. No reason to. It wasn't a convenient route between the main highway and the city. Plus, the gates were closed and locked by security guards every night. Only residents living within the safety of the tall wrought-iron gates and fences were given a code to enter after ten. It was one of the reasons I felt so safe living there—knowing that after a certain hour, people who didn't belong there couldn't be there.

The doorbell rang again. "Oh my gosh," I whispered to myself. "Jerry, what if something happened to one of the kids? You need to see who it is."

Kerry, at age thirty-five, had recently given birth to our first grandson, Noah, and was living with her husband in Milford. We were delighted to learn we were going to be grandparents. As Kerry got up there in age, we were starting to wonder if it would ever happen.

Our son, Kyle, was what we liked to call 'our adult child.' Just four years behind Kerry in age, Kyle raced dirt bikes most of his waking hours and financed his fun by working a security job at night. Jerry offered him a job at the PI office many times, but Kyle said working those hours took away from his time on the track. We always supported our children and the paths they had chosen for their lives, and racing wasn't any different. Kyle was a single guy with no kids, living on his own, and supporting himself with an honest living. Safe, happy, and healthy—all a parent could hope for. But no matter how old your kids get, when the doorbell rings in the middle of the night, it will create that knot in your stomach.

Jerry groaned and threw the blankets off. "Okay, I'm going to go check it out. I won't be able to go back to sleep anyway thinking someone could be hurt."

As he got up, I gave him a quick smack on the butt. I always loved how his butt looked in boxer shorts, even as an outline in the darkness. Patting his cute butt was something I'd done since he began courting me all those years ago. He gave me that shy little giggle that he never allowed anyone else to hear and told me, "Oh, you're gonna get it when I get back." Even with the dim moonlight shining through the curtains, I could see the gleaming bald spot that Jerry denied was on the crown of his head. It made me smile. I loved all his little imperfections.

He grabbed his old and tattered blue robe from the foot of the bed and wrapped it around his broad shoulders. While tying it closed, he used his foot to produce his brown corduroy slippers from under the bed. I watched as he started shuffling to the door. As he stepped into the hallway, I snapped back into the moment. "Take a bat with you."

"I would if we owned a bat, honey." He chuckled as he disappeared into the darkness.

I didn't know why I said that. I knew we didn't have a bat. But I was scared, and I didn't know why. We just didn't get people knocking on our door unannounced, let alone in the middle of the night. We should have owned a bat. Or one of those big mean dogs, like a Chow or Doberman

We had a dog. But our sweet little sixteen-year-old Maltese, Shadow, wasn't much of a deterrent for intruders. I had gotten Shadow from the rescue shelter on a whim after hearing Sarah McLaughlin singing on the TV with all those sad-looking cats and dogs flashing across the screen. I cried and cried and told Jerry we needed to save them. Jerry was allergic to cats, so I opted for the cutest little doggie that caught my eye. I called her Shadow because, in that shelter, she was so little and scared that she would take refuge in the shadow of the bigger dogs. And Jerry quickly came to love her as much as I did. He spent each evening sitting on the couch with her on his lap while he drank his beer and watched the news. But with her eyesight failing, she relied more on her hearing. Her bladder wasn't doing too well, so we kept her confined in the kitchen at night with a baby gate in the doorway and those doggie pee pads on the floor.

I reached toward the nightstand and turned on the lamp. It was much brighter than the illumination of the clock, and my eyes hadn't adjusted yet.

Not knowing what to do, I sat up straight, pulling the blankets up to my neck. I was worried. Nothing good happens at two in the morning.

I heard the faint creaking sound of the stairs as

Jerry walked down. I'd been wanting to tell him to fix those stairs for months, but he was so tired these days, and he'd been working so hard, I hadn't had the heart to bother him with it.

When I heard the front door open, the sound of low, mumbling voices traveled up to the second story and faded as they entered the room. The words were so quiet, I held my breath in an attempt to hear who it was and what they were saying. But all I heard was the bass tone of men's voices. Men. Was there more than one man ringing the bell, or was I hearing Jerry's as well? It was hard to tell.

Jerry was going to be so tired in the morning. He'd play it off and tell me he was fine, but he could never hide the bags and dark circles under his eyes when he hadn't gotten enough sleep. Maybe I'd make him that breakfast he liked so much, waffles with strawberries and whipped cream. *Do we have whipped cream? I'll make sure to check in the morning.*

I was tired, and my mind was wandering, so I got up and went to the window, hoping I could see who was out there. The night was clear enough to see all the stars in the sky, even with the streetlights on. I couldn't see the front door from the second story due to the overgrowth of the trees. It was the beginning of fall, and the leaves had just begun to take on their beautiful array of oranges and reds. But at this point, they hadn't started falling off just yet.

There was no car parked in front of the house, which I found odd. Not only was someone here at two in the morning, but they'd walked here? Something didn't feel right.

I tip-toed to the bedroom door and peeked my head out. The house was dark. Jerry hadn't bothered to turn on a light. Once my eyes adjusted to the darkness, I was able to navigate around the familiar house. I walked down the hall to the landing at the top of the stairs. The cool fall air filling the house from the open front door made goosebumps appear on my arms. Crossing my hands over one another, I gave myself a hug in an attempt for warmth. Good thing Jerry had put his robe on—he was always such a baby when he caught a cold. It was mid-September and probably in the low 50s. Fortunately, winter was not upon us just yet. I loved New Hampshire, but I hated the cold.

I leaned half of my body over the railing to get a look at the door, but with my belly just as big as Jerry's and my five-foot-four stature, I couldn't lean far enough to see who was there. The porch light shone in and illuminated Jerry's slippers on the old wooden floor. The murmured conversation had stopped.

"Jerry, who is it?" I finally called out in a whisper. He didn't answer back. The worry I'd felt when the doorbell rang had subsided, and fear had taken its place. Warmth began to filter through my body as my heart rate steadily rose. I could see that the heels of his feet were still. They were the only part of Jerry I could see because of the low-hanging ceiling.

Was someone lost and he was giving directions? I thought to go downstairs and see for myself, but not having a bra on under my nightgown made me feel uncomfortable around strangers. Especially male strangers. *Mental note: buy a robe for myself.*

What was going on down there?

"Jerry," I said a little louder and a lot more worried. Again, no answer. What the heck? I knew he could hear me. I just wanted to go back to bed. If I could go back to bed, that would mean everything was okay.

I worked part-time teaching at a school for special needs children. Mostly younger kids, seven to twelve years old. I loved teaching kids at this age— they were still receptive and eager to learn. Their special needs varied anywhere from autism to severe dyslexia. I used to teach full time, fourteen- through seventeen-year-olds, but as I got older, I had a hard time keeping up with them. Diagnosed with arthritis in my hands, the pain made it impossible to restrain the older, much bigger kids, from hurting themselves, as some of the special needs children often did. I truly loved my job and being with children, so with my sixtieth birthday fast approaching, I decided to move to part-time with the smaller kids instead of retiring altogether. I'd been incredibly happy with the transition.

I had work the next day too, but I didn't need as much sleep as Jerry. Or more like just wasn't as grumpy if I didn't get a full eight hours.

I knew I should just go back to bed. Jerry was obviously handling whatever was going on. He hadn't come back in for the phone, so 911 didn't seem to be a necessity.

Before heading back down the dark hallway, I leaned over the rail one more time and saw that

Jerry's feet were still planted facing the door. I was trying to listen for any kind of chatter, but I couldn't understand what was being said. It had only been a few minutes since Jerry answered the door. Too long for anything good to happen. With a sense of foreboding, I started backpedaling.

"Run."

I froze. I wasn't sure if that was what I heard, but I was sure of one thing—it was Jerry's voice. His tone was very matter of fact. And calm. Oddly calm for such a command.

I stood frozen with uncertainty, staring into the darkness of the hallway. The thumping from my chest grew louder with each passing second. For those few seconds, it was all I could hear. Then it came again, this time a lot louder: "Run." I wasn't confused by the order this time.

My eyes flinched, but I didn't move. I was frozen in place. My labored breathing quickly changed to frantic gasps for air. Grasping the sides of my head, I was trying to regain control of my own body. What did he mean, run?

Where was I supposed to run to?

It must have only been a second later when Jerry screamed, louder than I'd ever heard him, in a deep and unfamiliar tone that made me snap out of my paralyzing fear. "Cheryl, run!"

His words were followed by a loud thud and an exasperated exhale. The kind of sound one releases when getting the wind knocked out of them.

After taking a second to comprehend what he was

telling me to do, I hustled down the hall and into the bedroom. In my youth as a competitive swimmer, I would have had the ability to run. But at fifty-nine years old and two hundred pounds, that swimmer's endurance was long gone. I shuffled along as best I could. My knees and ankles ached at the unfamiliar need for rapid movement.

When I got into the room, I pushed the door forward, putting my hand between the door and the frame to ease it into the latch. *Click.* I didn't want whoever was out there to hear what room I'd gone into. I wanted to lock it, but I didn't want to lock Jerry out. I frantically looked around the room. There was nowhere else to run. Why did I need to run? "Oh god, what's happening?" I said aloud, though talking only to myself. I turned back and forth frantically, looking for somewhere to go.

The window.

As soon as I pulled the curtains back—*whack!* It came from downstairs and sounded painful. I looked back at the closed door. Men started yelling unintelligible words, followed by the stomping of heavy boots—fast-paced steps on the wooden stairs. More than one pair, and surely not the sound of Jerry's slippers.

They were coming. But who were *they*, and why were they inside of our house?

I need to call the police.

As I scrambled around the room in a panic, I remembered that we don't keep our cell phones in our room. As soon as Jerry left the force, he wasn't required to be available for callouts. So, to avoid disruption of any kind, we started leaving our phones in the kitchen to charge. I didn't think about needing them for an emergency of our own. I wasn't in the military like Jerry. I had never been deployed overseas like he was, and I'd never been up against an enemy like he was. But I wished I had some sort of basic instinct or training. Instead, I stood in the middle of the room doing nothing but praying. Clasping my hands together, I squeezed my eyes closed and silently begged God for safety. I begged for protection. I'd been a church-goer since I was a young girl and my faith in Him had grown into adulthood. I interlaced my fingers together and pleaded with the Man above.

I promise to read scripture every night. I promise to make the best of each day and see the kids more. Please God, just let us be okay.

Suddenly, the bedroom door was thrown open so hard that the doorknob smacked the wall behind it. White, flakey pieces of paint and drywall peppered the light tan carpet. I screamed at the unexpected entry. Jerry was thrown into the room by two men dressed in all black. They had hoods on, and their faces were covered by bandanas. One of them had a metal pipe or crowbar in his hand, I couldn't quite see in the shadows. Whatever it was, he was hitting it against his other hand with practiced dexterity. Like he was getting pumped up and ready to use it for something. Jerry had landed face-down at my feet as one of the men turned on the light.

"Oh my god, Jerry. Are you okay?" I kneeled next to him and brushed his messy hair back from his forehead. He hadn't started receding in the front just yet.

When he looked up at me without saying a word, I knew the answer. There was fear in his eyes. A look I'd never seen from him. Jerry didn't get scared. He was a man's man, a survivalist and a protector. At that moment, when he looked up at me from his place on the floor, I realized he could no longer keep me safe. Keep *us* safe.

Jerry tried to stand up, but one of the men used his boot to stomp on his back. An awful wincing escaped him as his body collapsed onto our bedroom floor. I held Jerry's face and looked up at the man. In an odd and incongruous moment, I noticed beautiful blue eyes peering above the top of his black bandana. They weren't your average color; they were a shade of teal that reminded me of the Caribbean Sea.

"Leave him alone. Stop what you're doing. Please," I begged.

"Cowards," Jerry uttered while trying to regain his breath.

Jerry was a proud man, and I knew he was trying to maintain his dignity while being forced face-down to his bedroom floor. His eyes bulged from their sockets and his nostrils flared as he looked up to the men in front of him. Continuous heavy sighs escaped him. These were no longer from the stomp to his back, these were different. Jerry wasn't used to being the victim, and it showed.

The other man—not the blue-eyed one, the short stocky one—was busy looking around our bedroom. Looking, but not touching or taking anything. He studied our trinkets and the knick-knacks that lined our dresser and shelves with souvenirs from my kids' travels abroad. When his eyes met our framed wedding picture, he stopped and stared for a few seconds, taking in our happiest day. In the picture, Jerry stood tall behind me with his black tux and cheesy grin, his hands on my waist. Like a picture from high school prom. His hair was thick then. He was thin in the right spots and muscular in the others. I wore a white lacy dress with long sleeves, capped right at the ankle. I'd chosen to forego the veil because I wanted to show off my professionally done hair and makeup. I clutched a beautiful bouquet of purple lilies in front of me, and it reminded me of how happy I'd been to be marrying him.

The man looked down at Jerry, then back at the picture. His voice was slightly muffled under the bandana, but I could understand him clearly. "Man, you actually married this fat bitch?"

Jerry pushed himself up to his feet, not giving the blue-eyed man enough time to force him back down. He tripped on his robe and made it only as far as his knees. Clenching his fists, he held them up in my honor. "Don't you ever. Ever. Talk about my wife."

Man, I'd thought I was at a decent weight in that picture. Thick, but not obese the way I ultimately became. *This man must really be disgusted by me now.*

While the guys were occupied by Jerry's bravado, I used the opportunity to look around for anything I could use as a weapon. Next to the clock on my nightstand, I saw my statue of Athena. She stood ten inches and was made of Alabaster stone. I slowly side-stepped toward the statue so as not to draw attention to myself. But I got anxious and before I was close enough, I leaned way over with my arm outstretched as far as it would go. It must have been too drastic of a movement, because the stocky guy spun around and glared at me. His dark brown, almost black, eyes peered above the bandana and were fixated on me. I saw the anger in those eyes even before he spoke.

"A fat bitch with balls, huh."

I didn't move another inch and I couldn't say anything. I mean, what could I say to that? Ashamed and embarrassed at being caught, I put my hands over my face and started sobbing.

He punched Jerry in the stomach, then pushed him aside, leaving him hunched over, holding his gut in pain. This had to be messing with Jerry's ego. Emasculation had never been something he'd had to deal with. I knew he'd been in plenty of fights with younger, stronger men, and come out on top. He always used to train with the youngsters he supervised in the Navy and with newbies in the department. *Keeps me prepared when guys of this age and stature come at me,* he'd said.

The man walked around the foot of the bed and stood in my face. I peered at him through my fingers. He stood several inches taller than me, about five-foot-eight—his stocky build must have made him appear shorter than he was. His deep-set almond eyes appeared vacant as they locked on to me with no emotion. My hands were shaking. I think I was expecting him to punch me in the same careless way he had done Jerry, so I braced myself.

That hit didn't come. Not yet, anyway.

Keeping his eyes on me, he reached over and picked up Athena. Through clenched teeth, voice slightly muffled by the bandana, he told me, "Try it again and you will watch your husband die." His tone was deep and stern, and I believed him.

He threw the statue to the floor, shattering it into pieces

"What do you want from us?" Jerry called out in angry desperation.

The blue-eyed man replied, "What I want from you is to shut the fuck up." Both men laughed. I continued to sob. This couldn't be happening. *Wake up, Cheryl. Wake up.*

2

WHEN THEIR LAUGHING STOPPED, I looked up from my hands, which were still cupped over my face. The men looked at each other. It was a look that told me each knew what the other was thinking. Then, without warning, the stocky guy grabbed me by my neck, spun me around, and wrapped his forearm around my throat. The pressure against my windpipe was immense. I grabbed at his wrist and tried to pull. His arms were thin, but strong. The choke-hold was blocking my ability to breathe, and I started to feel dizzy. My attempt to suck in air only caused my muscles to go limp. As my eyes shot around the room, the sight of familiar things faded away and turned into floating spots of light. Blackness would come, then the stars would appear again.

I fell to my knees, trying to scream as he lowered himself with me, maintaining the hold from behind. As Jerry tried to intervene, the blue-eyed guy grabbed him and put him in the same hold, then pulled out a knife and put it to Jerry's throat. "Move one inch, and this goes in."

Jerry stayed calm and didn't say a word. His eyes stared across the room into mine. He wasn't quiet because he was scared. He knew how to deal with life-or-death situations—his days of training and discipline were starting to show. He had been in countless such scenarios as a cop and during his deployments overseas—moments with details he never wanted to share. I knew Jerry would use everything in his power to get us out of there without getting hurt. I could see it in his eyes—he was coming up with a plan.

These men were trying to show us they were the ones in control. It was working. We were going to be submissive to them, and they were going to get whatever they wanted. This was the first time I had ever been threatened or touched in an aggressive way, and it was every bit terrifying as I might have imagined.

Holding his arm tight around my neck, the man whispered into my ear, "I doubt anyone would miss your fat ass. Shit, I doubt anyone will remember you after you're gone. You don't have one of those memorable faces."

Even though I was focusing on trying to stay conscious, all the foul language and name calling really hurt me inside. I'm a sensitive person, and I didn't like it at all. Tears flooded my starry vision. I tried to focus my attention across the room at Jerry, who still had a knife to his throat.

The stocky guy let go of my neck and told blue-eyes to go find some rope. When that squeezing pressure was finally released, I grabbed my throat and sobbed while inhaling as much oxygen as I possibly could. Deep, frantic gasps in; short, steady releases out.

The stocky guy pulled me up by stretching my arm to the extent of its reach. The blue-eyed guy let go of Jerry and told him to sit on the floor.

The man pulled me over to where Jerry was sitting on the floor, with his back against the bed. "Sit." It was a command. We were being ordered around like dogs who needed training.

"You're not tying us up. We'll stay out of your way, and you can take whatever you want, but you're not tying us up." Jerry was very matter-of-fact.

They didn't respond. The blue-eyed man, who stood about six feet tall, walked out of the room to find rope, and the stocky one closed the door behind him. I didn't know why. Was he about to do something he didn't want his partner in crime to know about? It was an odd thing to do otherwise.

He stared at Jerry and me sitting together on the floor. I hugged my knees into my chest. I held them tightly, hoping for improbable comfort. Jerry had his arm around my shoulders and was whispering, "It's going to be okay, my love." He sounded so calm and confident. But his assurance didn't make me feel any better.

The intruder glared at us and pulled down the bandana from his face with a slow and methodical motion. I squeezed my eyes closed and buried my face into my knees. With his voice stern and cold, he ordered me, "Open your eyes. Look at me."

I shook my head no. I knew what this meant. He was showing us his face because he didn't plan on letting us live to tell the police what he looked like.

He said it again. "Open your eyes and look at me." His voice was low, but angrier this time. I raised my head and took as much time as possible opening my eyes. I was hoping with this little delay, he would change his mind.

No such luck. I looked directly at him. He looked a lot younger now. Probably in his late twenties, with a clean-shaven baby face. He didn't look so scary without half his face covered.

He pulled the hood off, showing his short, curly brown hair. One curl fell out of place onto his forehead. Like Superman. How ironic. He was a handsome young man, but the anger on his face made him look tired. The kind of tired that implied he'd had a hard life.

"We won't tell," I whispered. "We won't tell anyone what you look like or what happened here. Just take what you want and leave, and we can forget this ever happened." My voice was quivering.

He laughed like we were pitiful. Then he spit in my face.

My reaction time in closing my eyes wasn't fast enough. Tears ran down my cheeks alongside the spittle.

Jerry yelled, trying to rise to his feet. "You fucking piece of shit."

The stocky man continued to laugh, then unexpectedly punched Jerry square in the face, quickly dropping him back down. I screamed and held Jerry's face in my hands. Bright red blood poured from his nostrils and over his lips.

He groaned in pain—or in anger, I wasn't sure which. Probably both. I used the back of my hand to wipe the spit from my face, then wiped it on the carpet. What were our tormentors planning next? I had a lump in my throat and was fighting back more tears. They'd liked when I cried earlier; I wouldn't give that to them again. I needed to toughen up. Play it smart. Give them what they wanted and try to get them out of here.

The stocky man smiled as we wiped spit and blood from our faces. It was a curiously asymmetric smile that pulled up one side of his face more than the other. But it showed an unapologetic joy.

I was still clueless as to what these men wanted from us. Had they really rung our doorbell in the middle of the night just to torture and torment us? Up until that moment, I had more faith in humanity than to believe that. *This is not just a burglary*, I thought, *these are people trying to destroy who you are as a person.*

"You don't know who I am?" The words shot through me like icy wind.

Were we supposed to? I wondered. I looked at Jerry, who was staring, trying to place him. I most definitely had never met this man.

I leaned over and whispered, "Jerry, you know this guy?"

"I don't know who the hell you are, buddy. I think you have the wrong people."

"Oh, you know of me, that's for sure. We've just never met face to face before. But rest assured, old man, you know me."

This guy was serious.

"Jerry, who is he?" I was shaking.

Jerry studied the man for what felt like a minute without saying a word. He was trying to place him. But how was he supposed to remember him if they'd never met? This was obviously someone Jerry had investigated, a suspect in one of his cases at some point over the years, but how was he expected to remember everyone he put away over such a long career?

The man saw the confusion on our faces. He pulled up the sleeve to expose his left forearm. It was some sort of tattoo, but at first, I couldn't see exactly what it was. There was no color, just black and gray faded against his pale skin. I leaned in a little closer.

A.C.A.B.

"What's it mean?"

"All Cops Are Bastards," Jerry educated me. "Is that supposed to help me remember you? Cause it's not ringing a bell. Most people I deal with hate cops, buddy."

The man pulled his sleeve back down again. Jerry continued, "Listen. I don't remember you. I'm not on the force anymore, so all the cases I had are shelved or worked by someone else."

The bully ignored Jerry's comment and went to the hallway and yelled for blue-eyes. "Hey man, where the fuck are you? If you can't find rope, just get duct tape or something. This is taking too long."

Taking too long? Maybe he was planning to tie us up, take what he wanted, and leave. Maybe the plan wasn't to kill us after all. The punching and spitting were just things he was doing to pass the time.

I whispered to Jerry, "Do you think they're going to leave after they tie us up? I want this to be over." I squeezed his arm for reassurance.

Jerry didn't even look at me when he replied. He started at the stocky man with disdain and said, "They aren't tying us up."

His voice was low and fearless. It gave me chills and, frankly, scared me. I loved that Jerry was always a brave man and had always made me feel safe. But his voice wasn't that of a husband and protector, not in that moment. He had vengeance on his mind.

"What do you plan to do?" I whispered. I felt my voice quaver. "Don't do anything stupid. I really believe they will kill us."

Jerry didn't say anything. He was plotting something. I didn't like it, and I was going to do something to prevent him from getting us killed.

"Um, excuse me," I said, loud enough for the man to hear me from where he was standing in the doorway. He didn't respond. I spoke louder, "Excuse me, mister. Sir."

"Damn bitch, what do you want?" he finally shouted back. It didn't bother me that he called me a bitch. It's amazing how fast you acclimate to abuse.

"I have a bad back, and sitting on this floor is causing me a lot of pain. Can Jerry and I sit on the bed?"

Jerry glared at me, "What are you doing, Cheryl? Let me handle this."

"First of all," the stocky one said, "stop calling me 'mister.' My name is Connor. And sure, if you can manage to lift your fat ass off the floor, you can sit on the bed."

Okay, I was wrong—that one still hurt. I knew I needed to lose weight. It was the first thing I was going to start working toward if I survived this night. But Jerry got up immediately, and helped me up as well. We sat down on the edge of the bed, still facing the man at the door. The man ... Connor. A wave of nausea came over me, and I felt myself starting to sweat. First, he showed his face, and now he was telling us his name. This was bad. This was really bad.

The blue-eyed man finally came back, but he was empty-handed.

"Where the fuck is the rope, Jason? Or the duct tape?" Connor was pissed.

Then it hit me. He'd not only told us his own name, he'd just given up his buddy's name—and Jason realized it too.

"What the hell man? You just said my name." Jason put his hands on top of his head and looked frantic. Pacing in small circles with panic in his voice, he rambled, "Why would you do that? Now these fat fucks are—wait. Where's your mask? You showed them your face too? You fucking idiot."

Jason threw his hands in the air, still moving about the room. His eyes, above his bandana, showed fear. It was the first time I saw one of them start to fall apart. I looked over at Jerry, and I was sure I could see a slight grin. I think he realized too—they weren't as together as they'd appeared.

"Dude, calm down," Connor told him. "Have you seen how weak these people are? They aren't going to the cops. They're too scared. And they should be." He pointed to us and laughed with a smirk on his face, but continued to talk to Jason. "Plus, we could kill them. Just to be sure. This old man is dead set on ruining my life, and I'm here to make damn sure that doesn't happen."

I believed he meant it. And I think Jason agreed with him too, because he stopped pacing. His hands dropped from his head to his face. "It will be a lot easier for him to ruin your life when he can see who you are, you idiot."

There was anger in Jason's voice. He sounded betrayed and confused.

After taking a few minutes to think, Jason ripped the bandana from his face and pulled the hood off as well. He was young. Not quite as young as Connor, maybe late twenties, but a lot younger than his deep, raspy voice had let on. He didn't have wrinkles or sun damage or any real signs of a rough life. He looked like an average young man I'd see bagging my groceries at the local market, and I was terrified of him.

"Listen, I'm totally down to help you, but when you start going against the plan, I feel like you're disrespecting me. And I don't like it." Jason sounded genuinely pissed off and stomped off toward the door.

Before making his way out, Connor grabbed his arm. "Listen, I'm sorry I didn't tell you what I was going to do. I just figured it doesn't matter if they see us or not. You know I can't let this dude walk."

Jason turned back and stared at Jerry, then back at Connor. "Alright, bro. But don't lie to me again." His anger with his friend quickly subsided. "We don't need to tie them up, we can lock them in that closet over there." He yanked Jerry up by his arm and started pulling him across the small room. I followed on my own, not wanting to leave Jerry's side.

Jerry didn't fight, but he kept asking Connor what this was about. "You have to understand, I don't remember all the cases I was assigned to over the years. You don't look familiar—maybe you've got the wrong detective or wrong precinct. I mean, I think I deserve to know since you are in my house."

Connor jumped up and down, seemingly excited at his friend being back on board with the plan. He didn't bother answering Jerry. His wide, toothy grin made him oddly cute. "Alright. Woo! Let's do this shit." He opened one side of the bi-folding doors while Jason pushed the back of Jerry's head, shoving him onto the closet floor. I voluntarily stepped inside to avoid being forced, and they shut the door. I could hear one of them messing around with the handles on the other side. I looked through the two-inch-wide horizontal slats and saw Jason take off his belt and wrap it around, holding the two doors tightly together. He gave a solid tug, ensuring we were locked in.

I heard them rummaging through our stuff. Drawers hitting the floor and things being tossed around. I wasn't sure what they were looking for, but we didn't have much in the way of valuables kept in our bedroom. Then I heard them walk into the hallway, and the whispers started. Presumably planning their next move.

Sitting there on the closet floor, I felt my hands trembling. I gave them a quick squeeze into fists, then released them. I was trying to get some blood flow going so the shaking would stop.

I reached over to Jerry for comfort, but he brushed me off and rose straight up to his feet. "We need to get out of here." He said it low and without fear.

"Out of here? This is the safest place we could be right now." That was the only thing I was confident about.

Jerry didn't reply. I felt his hand close into a fist as well. He wanted to break out of there. There were no windows in this closet, and the guys were still in the room. Whatever Jerry had planned would have to wait. And that's what we did ... waited and listened.

I heard Jason talking to Connor in a low voice, just above a whisper, but loud enough for me to hear the words.

"We aren't really going to kill them, are we?"

Connor's reply made me exhale with relief. "Naw, man. I just need to scare the fuck outta this guy so he stops looking for me."

"Okay, cool." Jason sounded like he was feeling as much relief as I was.

I whispered to Jerry, "We'll wait them out here in the closet. They just want to make sure we are afraid. Maybe if we just show them how scared we are, they'll leave sooner."

"Why don't you just leave? Be smart. The longer you're here, the better chance you have at getting caught." Jerry shouted through the doors.

I couldn't believe it. These guys had just basically said we were going to get out of this alive, and Jerry was provoking them.

I slapped Jerry's leg. "Shut up. What are you doing? You just heard them say they won't kill us, and you choose to poke the bear?"

"I want out of this closet."

"Yeah, so do I. Let them take what they want or whatever and leave."

This was the most Jerry and I had argued in our twenty years of marriage, and I didn't like it.

"You don't get it, Cheryl. He's here because he has some sort of vendetta against me. You think he's really just going to leave with your grandmother's good china?"

He was right. This was personal for Connor. We needed to know what the details of his crime were. Maybe a burglary or home invasion from way back when?

"What did they say to you at the door?" I wondered why Jerry hadn't yelled for help upon seeing two masked men in the night.

"I opened the door and was caught off guard by the two of them and how they were dressed. Connor

told me to step aside. That they were coming in.
His teeth were clenched, and he was whispering.
Presumably, so the neighbors didn't hear. I told them
that wasn't going to happen and to leave. I told them
if they left now, I wouldn't call the cops." I was getting
angry thinking of how this all came about. "I was
trying to keep you from hearing us and seeing them.
I told them I didn't have much cash in the house, but
they could take what I had. They weren't interested.
I was trying to stall in hopes they would leave. But
Connor had that metal pipe and used it to push me
back. That's when I told you to run." The guilt at
letting those assholes into our house seemed to set in.
His head dropped in shame.

"I'm so sorry, honey. I know there wasn't much
you could do." I put my head on his shoulder and
held his hand. I thought about the evening we'd had
before this ordeal began.

Jerry had gotten home from work and
immediately took up his place in the recliner. I
brought him a mug of cold beer that he swilled while
I prepared my family-favorite meatloaf, a recipe
passed down from my grandmother. I danced in
small steps around the kitchen while The Beatles sang
"Come Together" through Jerry's old transistor radio.

We ate on TV trays in the living room. Once the
kids grew up and moved out, we no longer saw the
point of sitting at a large dining room table. Besides,
sitting in front of the television was our bonding time.
We started out watching the news and listening to
the day's current events. Then, right at seven o'clock,
Jeopardy started. Jerry and I had friendly competitions

on who knew the most answers. Sometimes one of us gave a ridiculous answer that would send us both into a burst of deep, hearty belly laughter. Like tonight, when I said, "What is the titmouse?" for an answer about the softest rodent, forgetting that the titmouse is a bird. We had a good laugh about that, indeed.

We cleaned the kitchen together. I washed the dishes while Jerry dried. We were in bed by nine-thirty. Jerry was out as soon as his head hit the pillow, without a worry in the world. I stayed up for a bit reading *Christian Woman Magazine* and giving thanks for my wonderful life. Until all of that was taken away when the doorbell rang.

***

The room got quiet for what seemed like forever. The quiet scared me. I listened and waited, waited and listened, but all I could hear was the silence. That dreadful, still absence. I couldn't see them through the slats in the door, and I didn't hear any movement. The longer I listened, the more I heard my heartbeat. It was pumping hard, the steady rhythm of blood through my veins. The consistency of its pace was almost soothing.

Then the doorbell rang.

I flinched. My jaw fell open, and I felt a wave of nausea fill my stomach, rising to the bottom of my throat. "This can't be happening," I muttered under my breath. Did they have friends coming to join in on their torment? Or maybe one of the neighbors had seen Jason and Connor come in, and they wanted to see if we were okay?

"Jerry, let's start yelling. Maybe whoever is at the door will hear us and call the police. Maybe it is the police!"

Jerry didn't move, and he didn't say anything. He was now sitting next to me, squinting into our bedroom through a gap he'd created. I wondered if this was too much for him — if he was going into shock.

"Jerry," I said in a loud whisper. "Did you hear the doorbell ring?"

It seemed like almost a minute before he said anything. "Cheryl, the doorbell didn't ring. You were dreaming. You fell asleep, I'm guessing about thirty minutes after they locked us in here. You must have been dreaming about when this all started."

Asleep? How could I possibly have fallen asleep at a time like this? No way. I'd thought I was dreaming the last time it rang. And that sure as hell didn't turn out to be a dream.

"Are you sure the doorbell didn't ring? I know I heard a bell."

"I'm sure."

"But Jerry, I know what I heard, it was …"

"They killed Shadow," he interrupted. "They killed Shadow because she started barking. They have been downstairs throwing around the bell from her collar like it's a toy and laughing. They just threw it into our bedroom, and that's what woke you up."

"What the fuck do you mean they killed Shadow?" I'd resorted to cursing. The ladies at church would never have believed it. The Bible clearly states in several passages that cursing is an abomination. And I'd always believed there were better ways of getting your feelings across than using curse words. Yet here I was.

"Jason and Connor were going through our drawers. They took our wedding rings and talked about having them melted down for scrap metal. Well, with all the ruckus, Shadow kept barking. Connor said he was going to go shut her up." Jerry's voice was a monotone, and he didn't let on any emotion whatsoever. Way too calm for what he was telling me.

"Maybe he just put her outside in the backyard. Shadow couldn't have heard all that from up here. You must be mistaken," I said, hoping it was the case.

"I watched him. Connor took that crowbar or whatever he had in his hand when they came barreling in and stormed off downstairs with it. Once the sound of his boots faded away, I heard Shadow squeal one time. Just once. Her barking stopped. Then, all I've heard since then is her bell. No more barking, Cheryl … just the bell. They killed her."

Now I knew why Jerry looked like he was going into shock. Burglary and home invasion were one thing, but murdering our baby girl was quite another.

I had a hard time believing it. "But the guys said earlier that they weren't murderers. They're just dumb kids." I sobbed into Jerry's shoulder and thought of my little Shadow being bludgeoned to death in our kitchen. I imagined her cute little eyes looking up at these boys, hoping they would play with her. All she wanted was to play. I could see it—her little pink tongue hanging out, her tail wagging with excitement. Only to have her tiny head cracked open by much bigger animals.

The mental images were too much. I turned my head from Jerry and puked on my pile of shoes. I looked back at my husband, who now had his face in his hands.

This can't be happening.

3

Jerry wiped his tears and tried to stand up. The dangling clothes were lying on top of his head. He grunted in anger, and in his frustration, he ripped most of the clothes from the hanger, tossing them to the floor. Half of them buried my legs.

He wasn't crying anymore. He was angry. Instead, he started kicking at the doors and grasping onto the slats. Pulling, kicking, and screaming, "I'm getting us out of here" at the top of his lungs. I didn't know where Jason and Connor were, but Jerry didn't seem to care. He used both hands to clutch onto any part of those doors he could and kept kicking. The doors weren't designed to keep people out—or in—and they started to give. A few more kicks, and the wood splintered, allowing Jerry's foot to go through. The ends caught his leg, and blood ran down his shin onto his foot. He didn't care, maybe didn't even notice—he just continued to grunt and scream and thrash about until the hole was large enough for him to reach out and unhook the belt used to lock us in. What was left of the doors flew open at Jerry's last kick. I heard boots stomping quickly down the hall toward our room.

"They're coming," I said, trying to stand up. I had to use my hands to push my *fat ass* from the floor. My right hand went on top of my shoe pile and directly into my own vomit. I felt humiliated, again.

As I walked out of that closet, I was staring directly at the wall across the room. It only took me a second to realize that what I was looking at was blood. Smeared, bloody words across our white walls.

SHADOW WAS HERE

I screamed a god-awful howl and fell to my knees—where I puked again, so violently I felt my eyes straining in their sockets. I sat up with the chunks of last night's dinner mixed with bile dripping from my chin. Jason and Connor were now snickering from the doorway. Jason started a slow, sarcastic, clapping. "Bravo! You found a way to lose weight."

I collapsed in defeat. These men—these boys— were pure evil.

Jerry clenched his fists and ran at the boys. Just before he could throw a punch, Connor held up a photograph. It stopped Jerry dead in his tracks. It was a small, wallet-sized picture, but I couldn't tell who it was from my spot on the floor.

Connor held it right in front of Jerry's face, and Jerry fixated long and hard until the color left his skin. He turned pale and started swaying on his feet as if he were going to pass out. Connor smiled at Jerry's realization.

"Jenny. You're responsible for the disappearance of Jenny Wilson."

Suddenly I recognized it. He had taken the picture from Jerry's wallet. The corners were bent and worn, and the image had begun to fade.

The demise of Jerry's detective career had started three years ago, when Jenny's parents reported her missing after she didn't make it home from soccer practice. It was uncharacteristic of Jenny to be late like that, and she had never just *not* come home. Her teammates said the girl was leaving to meet up with a friend, but she hadn't mentioned who it was.

My mind started racing. There must have been some mistake. Maybe Connor had heard about the case and was showing off. I mean, it wasn't a secret that the perpetrator had never been found. The media and the Wilsons had made it all very public. Jenny's parents had provided Jerry and the news outlets with her most recent high school picture, a freshman photo. She was a beautiful and athletic-looking girl. The picture showed her standing in her soccer uniform, holding a ball under her left arm, her right hand proudly perched on her hip. She looked happy, the big grin on her face exposing her braces. Her long, blonde hair was pulled back into a ponytail, and her bright blue eyes appeared innocent and full of life. The picture was broadcast regularly on every local channel, day and night, with a 1-800 number to call with any information on Jenny's whereabouts.

I didn't know the girl. She wasn't from the area we lived in. But seeing her parents crying and begging on TV while holding their oldest child's photo was heartbreaking.

Connor chuckled and put the picture back in his

pocket. "That little teenage whore wanted everything that I gave her. She was a cock tease and needed to be taught a lesson."

I was wrong. Standing there in our home, in our bedroom was the guy. *The* guy from all that time ago. All the investigations and false leads. All the heartbreak and stress. The trauma and life-changing emotions. All of it now had a face. And a voice.

Jerry slipped out of his robe and lunged at Connor. They hit the floor, with Connor landing on his back, Jerry straddling his midsection. He started beating his face, but Connor just kept laughing as the blood poured out and spattered into the air with the rise of Jerry's white-knuckled fists. He did nothing but lie there and take it.

"You son of a bitch. You piece of shit. I'm going to fucking rip your face off."

All those years, Jenny's family had suffered, and so had ours. All the time, past and present, Jerry had put into looking for this guy—and he friggin' rang our doorbell.

Jason finally came over and squeezed Jerry into a tight bear hug from behind and pulled him up. Jerry continued to kick and swing, even when he was far from Connor's reach.

When he finally tired out, he just collapsed on the floor, panting. His bloodied knuckles dripped onto the tan carpet. I crawled to him and held him tight. He put his face in my neck and started sobbing. His warm tears ran down my skin, and I cried with him. Déjà vu from all those years ago.

In Connor's diabolical smirk, I could see blood pooled over his teeth. He spit toward his feet as Jason lifted him up. Jerry looked up just in time for Jason to punch him in the nose. The quick, percussive hit assured me that it was broken. Jason shook out his striking hand, and I realized he no longer had gloves on.

I looked at Jason in disgust. "That wasn't necessary."

Then I noticed blood spatter on his face and clothes. Dark red dots of a battle not yet over. I was confused at the dryness of it all. Not because of the spatter itself, but because he had only punched Jerry a few seconds ago. The blood shouldn't have been dry yet. Jason caught my stare. "See, Shadow *is* still with you." He burst out in laughter. "Cute name, too. I think I'll keep the collar as a parting gift."

I bit my lower lip as tears welled up in my eyes. "What kind of people are you," I uttered, feeling defeated and disgusted.

"You're about to find out," Connor answered as he pulled a heap of 550 cord from his pocket. Jerry had bundles of this braided cord in our garage left over from the military, so I immediately recognized what it was. Nylon, only about an eight of an inch in diameter, but super strong. From my understanding, it was used in the manufacturing of parachutes, and I'd seen Jerry use it in place of rope to secure large items many times. Larger items than us.

Jerry must have had that very thought when he saw Connor pull out the cord, because he stayed adamant to his earlier words. "You're not tying us up." His bellowing echoed between our bedroom walls and returned a painful ring to my ears.

Jason wasn't nearly as taken aback as I was. He moved close to Jerry's face, nose to nose. "That's exactly what we're going to do. And I'm getting really fucking tired of you trying to play this tough-guy role. You're no tough guy. You can't even protect your own fat wife from strangers in the middle of the night."

He was painting Jerry to be this disgustingly impuissant man. And that wasn't my Jerry. That wasn't who Jerry was at all. In fact, he was the opposite.

"You should have left it alone," Connor uttered. "All those years ago, I sat watching you and that bitch's family on the news, asking for help finding me. You people didn't have a clue. I watched and laughed. My life went on. That is, until recently, when I heard you found that guy on the boat. The guy who told you he saw me with that Jenny bitch by the water. You just had to start poking around again, didn't you? I told that fuckin' guy to mind his own business or I'd hunt him down. Staring me down like he was going to do something. But with that pretty little girl sitting port-side, he didn't want to risk it. I knew I should have taken care of him then. That was my bad."

Jerry appeared stunned. I didn't know how Connor knew about this new witness, because I sure didn't.

"Jerry, what's he talking about?" I thought he told me everything.

He turned from Connor and gave me that look

that said *I'm sorry*. Then he explained how he'd started asking a lot of questions around the docks again recently. Near where Jenny had been known to be. There was this guy on a boat, a real fisherman type with a long beard and slickers Jerry hadn't seen the first times around. He approached Jerry at the tackle store and told him he had some information about Jenny. Said he was afraid to come forward back then because some guy had threatened him, and he had his daughter with him. But his little girl was off living with her momma now, so he felt it was time to tell what he saw.

"I can't believe you didn't tell me you found a witness. After all this time." I felt hurt.

"I'm sorry, honey. But I didn't want to get your hopes up. I wanted to wait and see if what this guy was telling me was true." He sounded disappointed in himself.

"That makes sense." It did make sense to me. We had a lot of let-downs back then. I could see why he hadn't wanted to get too excited just yet. I thought back to the case. I needed a way to comprehend how we got to his night. Figuring out why we were in this mess might help us get out of it.

4

IT WOULD BE HARD TO OVERSTATE how difficult things were then. I remember Jerry saying the tracking of Jenny's cell phone was unsuccessful because the phone had been turned off. Cell phone tower records showed Jenny's last known location as being at Lederman Park, where she'd had soccer practice. Not far from the docks.

The Wilsons had scoured the area, and any locations Jenny was known to visit—the mall where she would sometimes meet up with friends and the local arcade where she would use her loose change to play air hockey. Both turned up empty. It seemed she had just vanished without a trace.

Due to the suspicious circumstances of a child's disappearance, Jerry was assigned the case. Historically, when a child went missing in Boston, the police department put their best investigator on it, and he was their best.

The next morning, Jerry began at Jenny's school, asking her friends and classmates for any information—after all, teenagers typically tell their friends more than they tell their parents. He heard rumors that Jenny had a boyfriend her parents weren't aware of, an older boy who had reportedly dropped out of high school years prior. Many students told some version of this story, but not even her closest friends had ever met the boy or knew his name.

Jenny's best friend, Cara, said Jenny once showed her a picture of the boy she claimed as her boyfriend. Cara described him as, "too cute to be real," telling Jerry, "The picture she showed me looked like it was pulled from the internet. He appeared to be a model or something. And he had a little bit of facial hair. Definitely older. I knew she was lying, but I didn't call her out on it."

Girls often get jealous of each other. Especially when it comes to boys. It sounded like Cara only thought Jenny was lying because the boy was so good looking. That was how Jerry took it.

Prior to Jenny's disappearance, everyone she knew said she appeared to be happy and carefree; she hadn't shown any signs that her life was anything but ordinary.

"Hell, she'll be fine," Jerry confidently told me over dinner. He expected the typically obedient girl was just acting out, as many teenagers do. She'd probably met up with the boy and was now afraid to come home for fear of punishment from her parents. He'd seen cases like this many times before.

He told the Wilsons what he'd gathered from the kids at school and assured them she would probably be walking in the door any minute.

Jerry never made promises he wasn't sure he could keep. That was the kind of man he was, and I loved that about him. Plus, it was his gut feeling, and when it came to Jerry, his gut instincts rarely failed him. It was one of the many reasons he had always been so successful at his job—he had that knack for people and behaviors. He could immediately tell when he was dealing with a bad egg or just someone who'd simply made a mistake. And all signs showed that Jenny was probably just out sowing her wild oats. A good kid, but a teenager none-the-less.

But when the days passed and Jenny had been missing for almost a week, the local news stations ran the story. The headline had read:

Local 14-year-old Jenny Wilson Missing.

Jerry's confidence at Jenny's reemergence turned into disbelief. When first assigned the case, he'd dismissed any thought of foul play. I mean, why wouldn't he? His instincts had always been right— until now.

Jerry began pacing around the house with his hand covering his mouth, shaking his head. He would ask questions out loud, then answer himself. *I should have known better. I knew in my gut something wasn't right, yet I let it go. I was so sure she would wander home at any minute, I didn't bother to look much further. Why would I do that? Why would I rely on assumptions instead of looking for facts?*

Desperation and despair had been apparent. The unfocused gazing at the walls, the stuttering and inability to make complete sentences, his once-confident posture replaced by slumping, his head

43

hung low. I remember it so vividly because in front of me was a man I didn't recognize. Because for the first time in his career, he was skeptical of his own decision-making.

The phones at the police department rang off the hook with tips and leads. Jerry followed up on every single one of them, no matter how crazy some of them sounded. Each night Jerry came home, he would tell me about the craziness of the calls. One caller said he'd seen a girl he believed to be Jenny working in a strip club in Los Angeles—three thousand miles away from Jenny's home. Just a week before, Jerry would have laughed at that call. It seemed far-fetched given the type of person everyone said Jenny was and the close, loving family she came from. But he couldn't rely on his past successes and experiences anymore. He'd begun to question everything he thought he knew about detective work. Not to mention, human trafficking had become such a national crisis. So, he called the Los Angeles police department and sent them the photo and had them check out that club anyway, just to cover every base.

When the L.A. officer called back to say no one there had seen Jenny, Jerry was kind of let down. Not that he wanted her to have been dragged off across the country; but because if she were there, it would have she could be taken home.

Jerry and I spoke during that time about how terrified the Wilsons must have felt. We had two children of our own, all grown up already; I couldn't bear the thought of something so atrocious happening to one of them. To imagine it was sickening.

Each night, Jerry came home more and more frustrated at the complexity of the case. Jenny had last been seen walking home from soccer practice, then vanished into thin air. That was it. Jerry knew from his experience that people don't just vanish. Someone always knows something, and there is always some sort of clue. But not this time. The case went against everything Jerry knew about crimes and missing persons, and it was driving him crazy. People don't just vanish. He wasn't sleeping or eating. He wasn't taking on new cases like he was supposed to. His boss, Lieutenant Hammond, was riding him hard. And the mood swings ... those were the worst of it. On his days off, he was barely talking to me, or anyone for that matter. I loved and respected how much he cared. He had a heart of gold—he was dedicated, trying his hardest to uphold his promise to the Wilsons. But it was rough to deal with.

Then, one Sunday afternoon, one month after Jenny was reported missing, the phone rang. Sunday was football day, and Jerry was stretched out in his recliner with beer in hand, watching the Steelers work their way to the next Super Bowl. I knew better than to think he would get up to answer the phone, so I picked up the landline in the kitchen. I wasn't surprised to hear Jerry's partner, Detective Seamus McCarthy, on the other end. Having been married to Jerry for almost twenty-five years, I'd learned his work never ends. Not for weekends, not for holidays, and surely not for football.

"Hi Seamus, you sure are brave calling during the Steelers game," I laughed. Seamus had been Jerry's partner for ten years and was like family to us. When he didn't respond with his normal joke about how the Steelers suck and it's all about the New England Patriots, it caught me off guard.

"Cheryl, get Jerry for me." His tone was flat and sounded very official, which made me nervous.

"Is everything okay?" I was starting to worry.

"Just get Jerry, please."

I didn't push it any further. Whatever he had to talk about was obviously not worth delaying.

"Jerry, Seamus is on the phone."

"What the hell are you doing Roethlisberger, throw the damn ball," Jerry cursed at the quarterback through the TV.

"Seamus wants to talk to you, and he doesn't sound right," I yelled from the kitchen,

"That bastard knows his team is winning and is calling to gloat. Tell him I'll call him back. This game isn't over yet. And tell him to be prepared to make good on his bet when we win." I'd always wondered why Jerry said *we* when referring to his favorite team. My guess was it boasted him up. Probably made him relive the football days of his youth as a star linebacker.

I set the receiver down and went to the living room. "Hon, I don't think he's calling about the game. Something is wrong."

Jerry stared at me for a second, presumably to see if I was messing with him or not. Seamus loved messing around with Jerry during football season. Their banter about which players and which team were better was usually nothing short of hilarious. But when he saw my face, he realized I was serious.

After setting his beer down on the table, Jerry pulled the handle to lower the recliner's legs and popped up from his seat. I followed him to the kitchen so I could eavesdrop. Even though it was normal for Jerry and Seamus to get callouts on their days off, I had never heard Seamus sound the way he did. It was different this time. His tone was taut and low.

"Talk to me, man." Now Jerry sounded official. I normally found his work talk very sexy, with all the codes and cop slang. *10-4* or *copy that* were most common. It made him sound authoritative and in control. But with something clearly going wrong, I didn't feel it this time.

Jerry stood there listening, staring at the wall while Seamus gave him information I couldn't hear. I started chewing on my fingernails with anticipation of the unknown. What was so different about this callout from all the other hundreds of times?

"Shit. I'll meet you there in thirty minutes," he said before hanging up the phone.

"What is it, Jerry? What's happened?"

"Some jogger found Jenny's cellphone by Bass River. I have to go."

"Of course, go." I held his face in my hands and kissed his cheek before he went running out the door.

***

I remembered hearing the front door open at eleven that night. It startled me because I had inadvertently fallen asleep on the couch waiting up for Jerry to get home. I knew how much the case meant to him, and I wanted to hear about what was going on.

At first, I was confused by my husband's demeanor. He sighed his usual sigh to let me know he was exhausted. Then, when he stepped down into the living room from the entryway, he threw his badge on the floor. The tin shield bounced along the carpet and came to rest at the foot of his old, supple leather recliner. I was perplexed. Then, once he started laughing and crying at the same time, I was disquieted. He kept up the pattern for a few minutes at least. Laugh hysterically, then sob into his cupped hands, all while pacing in small circles, pulling his hair straight out from his head. Then I put it together.

"Oh no. Please tell me it's not what I think it is."

He stepped over his badge and sat down without pulling the foot elevation up as he typically did. Using the backs of his hands, he wiped at his tears, like a child when Mommy tells them it will be okay. The hysteria had stopped. He didn't answer me, but he didn't have to.

"She's dead?" I asked, already knowing the answer.

His lack of response was all I needed as confirmation. "My god, her poor family. How? Where?" He didn't look at me. With his hands over his face, he sobbed like a parent who had just lost his own child. I knelt in front of him, placing my shaking hands on his knees. "Honey, what happened?"

There was a knot in my stomach. I couldn't believe it. I thought for sure she would turn up alive and well. Nothing led us to believe otherwise.

Jerry sat up and tried his best to gain his composure. "Her body was found near Harborwalk Terrace. Just around the way from where her cell phone last pinged." He paused for a second, which gave him time to choke back tears. "She was naked, and her body had started to decompose. She was wearing nothing but her tennis shoes. Her right hand was closed into a fist, most likely from fighting her attacker. I tried to open it, but with rigor mortis causing her body to be so rigid and stiff, it was too difficult. Her soccer uniform was located nearby, partially buried under some brush. Only thing missing was her phone. Whoever did this was sloppy. And I'm going to find the son of a bitch."

"Oh my god, honey. I'm so sorry." I held him tightly as we cried together. I waited a few minutes before I asked, "What happens now?"

Jerry wiped his tears with his sleeve, then pulled his hanky from his pocket to blow his nose. "The lab will process her body for any physical evidence. Swabbing for DNA, looking for any clues, things like that."

He looked at the floor in shame before telling me, "When I went to notify the Wilsons … I—I could only say that I was sorry. I couldn't tell them, 'Your daughter is dead.' I just couldn't say the words. But Mrs. Wilson knew what I meant. I mean, for the first time, I couldn't even look her in the eye. She stood there staring. Waiting for an explanation. When I didn't say another word, she slapped me across my face so hard it made my teeth hurt. All I could do was clench my jaw and bear it. I deserved it. Mr. Wilson came to the door. He said they'd trusted me. They'd believed me when I said just give it a little time and she'd come walking through that door. All I could utter again was that I was sorry. He slammed the door in front of me and I heard this god-awful, gut-wrenching scream from inside. The kind of scream you only hear when a mother is told her child is dead. I failed them, Cheryl."

5

IT BECAME JERRY'S PRIMARY RESPONSIBILITY to find out what had happened to Jenny and why.

With the frustration of working the case came determination. Jerry was still barely sleeping or eating, and it only got worse. His mood was absent toward me at best. But I didn't take it personally. He'd always treated me so well. Never as much as raised his voice at me. And even with his moods, he was always kind and always kept me informed on what he was doing.

With every lead that came, a letdown followed. Jenny didn't have enemies. She was a B student, had good friends, and wasn't involved in anything crazy like gangs or drugs. Hadn't even dabbled in marijuana or the new vaping trend like most teens were doing. She was your average teenage girl and the star of her high school soccer team. It seemed to be a senseless, unprovoked crime. No evidence of any secret boyfriend could be found. It seemed the kid at school was right; she'd probably made up the boyfriend to sound cool or gain attention. Sometimes kids did that, I guess.

Jerry thought about our own daughter and how thankful he was that she had grown up to be safe, happy, and healthy. Our son too, of course. But Jenny reminded Jerry so much of our Kerry that it caused him more guilt.

He put his heart and soul into that case for two straight years. It was an emotional roller coaster for both of us, and his drinking became more frequent. His attempt at trying to numb it away just wasn't working. All it was doing was preventing him from moving forward with life. Never an angry drinker, my Jerry—just a quiet one.

***

It was three months from the time Jenny's body was found to when the call came from the forensic crime lab. The results were bittersweet. Male DNA had been located under Jenny's fingernails, on her clothes, and spread across her neck and thighs. However, there was not a hit in the FBI's Combined DNA Index System, or CODIS, as Jerry referred to it. Jerry explained that CODIS was a national databank with DNA on file for people who had been arrested for felony crimes. So, whoever this guy was, he was a disgusting piece of shit who had somehow managed to avoid ever being arrested. Jerry explained that the lab would hold the results should the DNA ever need to be compared with anyone in the future.

The lab also revealed that Jenny's hymenal tissue had been broken and there were signs of vaginal trauma. Evidence of sexual assault. No semen had been found, so the perp may have worn a condom, or simply pulled out prior to ejaculation. The autopsy had yielded another clue. Clutched tightly in the hand Jerry couldn't pry open on scene was a necklace. A silver rope chain with the Irish Claddagh charm hanging in the center. The Claddagh, in Irish culture, represents love, loyalty, and friendship, displayed by two hands holding a heart with a crown on top. Jenny's parents said the necklace didn't look familiar and it wouldn't make sense for her to wear something like that, since Jenny was a mix of English and Swedish descent, not Irish. But the odd thing was the chain was very thin and dainty, feminine looking.

New female DNA had been located on the necklace, along with more from the same male. But no CODIS hit for the female either. The necklace was a lead that Jerry was excited about.

But after two years of searching and working tirelessly, there were no more leads. Video surveillance all around Harborwalk and Lookout Terrace showed thousands of people coming and going from the popular waterfront location. But nothing on those videos caught the eye of anyone on Jerry's detective team. It seemed almost impossible Jenny could have been dumped there without any video capturing it, but that was what had happened. Jerry said it was possible the perp had come in through one of the cameras' blind spots.

The anonymous false tips quit coming in— along with any promising ones. The case officially went cold, and Jerry was instructed by Lieutenant

Hammond to put the case in storage and move on to the other ones that had since piled up on his desk. "I can't just drop it, boss," Jerry told him. And he refused the order. Each day he went to work early and stayed late, going over the case from beginning to end.

One day, I stopped in to bring Jerry dinner at the office and he was just standing there, staring at this wall. My mouth fell open at all the photographs and post-it notes woven together by pieces of yarn. Different-colored thumbtacks were scattered across a map of Boston, stretching from Fenway Park to Castle Island. Jerry's dress shirt was untucked and sweat stains showed under his arms. That was also when I noticed that he hadn't been shaving. Gray stubble covered his usually smooth face. He looked ill and worn out. But how could I tell him to quit? If Jenny had been my child, this would have been exactly what I would hope the detective on the case would do.

I set his Tupperware on his desk and simply said, "If you're not mentally sound, you're not going to be productive." He didn't reply, and he didn't need to. I hugged him around his waist from behind and told him I loved him.

That night, he came home and found me sleeping on the couch. I never felt right going to bed without him. So, when he worked late, that was where I slept, until he would come home and wake me for bed. But on that night, after his boss had told him to move on and I dropped off his dinner, he said he did some soul searching. The whole case had taken such a toll on him, and he decided that he'd had enough. Enough of seeing all the horrible things in life. Questioning himself and his capabilities as a detective, he thought maybe he was too old to be doing this line of work now. That mental sharpness that made his colleagues envious was now gone. He felt defeated.

Sitting at his desk, he stared at the pile of case files waiting to be opened. Each was going to have its own story and horrid details. He became overwhelmed with the thought of more families like the Wilsons in those files. More families to let down. More tragedy and less justice. At that moment, Jerry resigned from the department without ever opening another file. He looked at Jenny's soccer photo pinned to his board. It was too much to bear. He pulled the pin from the picture's edge and slid it into his wallet. He walked out, taking nothing else with him.

To this day, he still carried that photo in his wallet. The very picture Connor would one day hold up in Jerry's face.

6

ONLY A FEW MONTHS OFF THE JOB, Jerry was going
stir crazy at home. He wanted to work. He needed
to. He'd planned on doing police work until he
physically couldn't handle it, but he wasn't expecting
that final homicide to take away all his emotional
energy and confidence. No other case he had worked
in the years prior had hit him as hard as Jenny
Wilson. Before, he was so self-assured. Even the cases
he lost at trial he didn't take to heart, because he
was always confident that he had done everything
in his power and left no stone unturned. He did
everything by the book, and he was proud of that.
Never tampering with evidence or falsifying a report,
Jerry had a stellar reputation at the department. Not
everyone who worked at Boston PD could say the
same about themselves.

To get back into some sort of work, he took a part-
time job as a private investigator. It was just what he
needed at that time in his life. Wanting to help people
was part of his nature. But two years sitting at a desk
had taken a toll on his physical capabilities. You see,
the PI work didn't require a fitness test or chasing

after crooks on the streets. It was more stakeouts and computers, which allowed for Jerry to put on the spare tire around his once rock-solid midsection. I never said anything to him about the weight gain. I was proud of him. I just replaced his clothes with larger sizes and started preparing healthier meals for him.

Then, last month, two years after leaving the department, Jerry came home from work in an abnormally chipper mood. I was in the kitchen chopping onions for dinner, a ground turkey meatloaf I proudly made from scratch. Whistling and smiling, he kissed me on the cheek before grabbing his beer from the fridge.

"It seems that someone had a good day. Did you locate another cheating husband?"

Last time he'd come home from work this happy, it was because he'd finally tracked down a husband who had a long-time mistress. The guy had set the girl up in an apartment and was pretty much leading a double life. Infidelity angered Jerry. He didn't understand it. He was a loyal man. His motto was, *If you want to be with someone else, just leave.* So, in his new line of work, he felt very satisfied and validated by catching the cheats. It was only when the spouses requested all the unflattering details that Jerry had a hard time with it. He didn't like to be the cause of anyone's pain, even if it truly wasn't his fault.

"Nope. No cheaters found today, *but* I came up with a great idea." He popped the cap off his beer and poured it into a large mug. "I was sitting at my desk, hungry, as I usually am, and decided to order a pizza instead of eating that healthy crap you put in my lunchbox—no offense, honey."

I wasn't offended. It was my subtle attempt at trying to get him to eat better.

"Anyway, when the pizza guy got to the office, I took out my wallet to give him the tip and Jenny Wilson's picture fell out. It landed on the old carpet at my feet, next to my many coffee stains. I just stared at it. I hadn't looked at her picture since that night. That night I left the PD. It was too hard. And now there it was—there *she* was. Smiling in her soccer uniform. The last clothes she ever wore. It felt like a punch in the gut."

I was confused, because seeing her picture after all this time had obviously struck a nerve, but his excited demeanor didn't match with that. He picked up a handful of diced tomatoes from the cutting board and popped them into his mouth. I stopped chopping.

"I can imagine how difficult that must have been, sweetie. But I'm not understanding all of this." I pointed at his ungraceful gliding around the kitchen.

"I'm going to re-open Jenny's case."

My heart fell into my stomach as I tried to absorb what he'd just said. "You're going to what?"

"It's perfect. I have the time to focus on the one case now. I can go back to the files with a fresh perspective. To try and bring some closure for the Wilsons. No one at Boston PD has looked at that file since I left. It's time to solve this, Cheryl."

He said it as if it shouldn't come as any surprise. Then he took his beer to the living room and took his place in his recliner, as he did every evening. But when he picked up the remote and clicked on the TV, I had to interject. I stepped in front of the screen and pushed the button to power it off.

"Why now?" I asked. "What's going to be different in those files that you didn't already see?" I had gotten my Jerry back, and the thought of him sliding back into that sinkhole of depression he'd been in while working the case scared me.

"I need to know—her family needs to know what happened to her. Seamus is still on the force and can help me with anything I need from the department."

An uneasy feeling came over me. I didn't want to go through that again. I couldn't go through that again. All the silent treatments and lack of intimacy. Hugs, kisses, and hand-holding nonexistent. Jerry not eating for days at a time. Not taking phone calls or visits from the kids. And the mood swings. God, those were the worst of it.

"I can't stand by and watch you deteriorate again, honey. And I sure won't tolerate the way the kids and I became second to this insatiable need for closure. I just won't do it." I stormed out of the room like a pouting teenager.

***

That night in bed, I lay next to Jerry and stared at the tranquil look on his face as he slept. I pondered over the past. Sure, Jerry had become a depressed mess when Jenny's case went cold. But for good reason.

He'd gone against his own training, and for the first time, his instincts were detrimentally wrong. And the Wilsons—they never forgave him for giving them hope.

I decided my fears were selfish ones, so I buried them inside and supported his decision. After all, any parent in the Wilsons' shoes deserved to have answers.

As the sun rose in the early morning hours, Jerry opened his eyes to find me fixated on him. "Good morning. Surprised you're awake already."

"I didn't sleep. I was thinking about you re-opening Jenny's case." Jerry started to cut me off, but I put my pointed finger over his lips and continued. "I understand why you need to do this. I love you and want to support you, but I have one condition. This time around, you don't shut us out. Not me, and not the kids. Understood?"

Jerry's face lit up like a kid on Christmas morning.

"Thank you, baby! Thank you so much. And this time, I assure you, it will be different." He grabbed my cheeks with both hands and planted little kisses all over my face.

And just like that, the case was re-opened.

7

"I COULDN'T RISK YOU FINDING ME. So, I found you first," Connor said with a smirk. He was proud. His goal was to find us—to find Jerry. And he had accomplished that.

Jason threw in his two cents, "And because he decided to find you first, here I am, meeting you lovely people."

His sarcasm had a trace of annoyance. That annoyance quickly turned to anger, as Jason head-butted Jerry directly in the already-broken nose. The impact sent blood droplets spraying into the air. My husband snapped backward to the floor, rolling from side to side while cupping his hands over his face.

I screamed for Jason to stop. I begged. My screams fell on deaf ears as the man began punching him. Over and over, Jason's long arms stretched back to obtain full velocity. The punches only stopped when Connor used the crowbar like a golf club, full swing to Jerry's right knee. Jerry's shriek was unbearable. His cries sounded like those of a little boy, high-pitched and pre-pubescent. Jerry was a man's man. He fished, chopped wood, changed the oil in our cars—and now, he couldn't defend himself or his wife. I was sure he was feeling his manhood was nonexistent at this point. But to me, nothing could be farther from the truth. He was doing all he possibly could given the situation. There were two against one. They were much younger and had a weapon. Not an even fight by any means.

I curled up on my side and held my knees to my chest. A defenseless child in the fetal position. I squeezed my eyes shut and covered my ears, praying to my Lord and Savior for the horror to end.

Then a loud thud, followed by Connor's voice. "J—, we aren't going to be able to get this fucker downstairs. Let's just do this shit here, in their bedroom. This is where the 'magic' happens for them anyway, right?" He chuckled, and I opened my eyes.

Jason looked around the bedroom and thought for a second. "Alright, man. This is the spot."

The spot. Do what "shit" right here? My mind raced as I tried to get one step ahead and thwart their plan before it could begin.

Before I could think of answers to my own questions, Jason grabbed a clump of my hair from behind and wrapped it around his fist. He pulled me from the fetal position back onto my knees. Attempting to ease the pain, I reached up with both hands to loosen his grip. But there was no way that was happening. I looked to the side of the bed where Jerry was facedown with Connor stepping on the back of his neck. I realized the *thud* I'd heard was Connor knocking him down.

Jason instructed, "Dude, sit him up. Pull him to the foot of the bed and tie his hands around the post near the floor."

Connor followed his directive.

Jerry made these god-awful bubbling sounds as the blood from his broken nose ran down the back of his throat. Struggling to talk, he gurgled, "You're not tying us up." I think he was in so much pain that he didn't realize he was already tied up. His right leg was outstretched in front of him, and the disfigured swelling of his knee showed the cap was now more on the inside of his knee instead of in the front where it was supposed to be. His left leg was pulled inward, knee to chest. He laid his head forward, resting his forehead on his knee.

"You do realize if he passes out from pain, this whole thing is fucked, right? You didn't have to take his knee cap off." Jason was obviously irritated with Connor flying off the handle.

"Oh, my bad. I didn't realize we were here to coddle these fuckers," Connor shot back sarcastically before leaving the room. "I'll be right back—don't nurture them too hard while I'm gone," he yelled from down the hall.

Jason was pulling my hair tighter now. I felt strands being ripped from my scalp every time he moved. Not in a clump, just a few strands at a time. My hands remained on his, hoping there was some small chance I could at least relieve a little of the pressure. I wished I would have exercised more or eaten healthier. I should have made some of those healthy lunches for myself too. Not because they keep calling me fat—well, maybe because of that too—but because I didn't even have the strength to defend myself. I couldn't even budge his one hand with two of my own. Looking at Jerry tied to the bed with his hands behind his back, his face still resting on his good knee, I realized they were right—*we are pathetic*.

I couldn't help but dwell on how we got here. How we allowed these two terrorists to enter our home. We were so naive to think we lived in a safe bubble just by being in some gated community. They said they weren't murderers, then bludgeoned my poor Shadow to death. *Oh god. I can't believe she's gone.* I tried to fight back tears. But that didn't last long when I pictured my poor little soft white furry baby, dead in this house somewhere. The flood gates were open.

"Shh, stop crying. Connor is sorry he broke your husband's nose. And even though he's not showing it, he's sorry he broke his knee too. He tends to go a little overboard sometimes."

Jason's voice was low and soft. It sounded so genuine I almost believed him.

"I bet right now, Connor is getting him some ice and maybe even some pain meds if you have them."

"Really?"

"Yeah. He's pissed your ol' man started looking for him again, I guess. So, I think he just wants to make sure he stops going after him."

He let go of my hair. I didn't realize it was the tension of the pull that had been keeping me upright until he let go and I fell forward. I should have known

I didn't have the core strength to sit straight like that for so long. My head started pounding with the relief of the pressure. I groaned while gently rubbing the roots of my missing strands of hair.

"Cheryl, are you okay?" Jerry looked up from his resting position. His voice was oddly cold, but still caring. I could hear the anger beneath it, though. Not with me, but with the situation.

No, I am not okay. I woke up to these vile men invading my home, I was locked in a closet where I puked on my shoes, I put my hand in that same vomit, my dog was murdered, my hair ripped from my head, and I'm still sitting next to a pool of my own vomit on my bedroom floor.

That's what I wanted to say. But I looked at Jerry and his broken nose and disfigured knee and felt horrible for even thinking that.

"Yes, honey, I'm hanging in there. We will be okay."

I turned to our captor. "Jason." This was the first time I'd addressed him by name. Since he was now being somewhat humane, I thought deep down that maybe he had some empathy and kindness, the kind that was clearly lacking in Connor. Maybe he was a decent guy normally, but might have gotten into drugs that changed who he was. I saw this special on the news once where they said the use of methamphetamines had become all too common, that they can make users agitated and angry. If he was using meth, maybe he was high when they got here and it was wearing off now. That had to be it. And his response to me calling him by name further proved my theory.

"Yeah, what's up?"

No *bitch* at the end? I was right, he was back to his normal self. I felt a twinge of happiness and hope. Respect them, and they will respect you—I learned that when I was getting my teaching credentials at the University of New Hampshire.

"Jason, if you boys are hungry, there's some leftover meatloaf in the fridge. And I think there's pop in another fridge, out in the garage."

He put his hand on my shoulder. Gently. Not the rough way he had been handling me.

"No thank you, I ate earlier. We shouldn't be too much longer. It's going to be daylight soon."

I looked at the bedside clock. I couldn't make it out from where I was. Squinting and trying to focus didn't help. Jason must have realized what I was looking at. He glanced at his watch. "It's about 4 a.m."

"Thank you." I was thanking our captors now. But I meant it. I was appreciating his newly displayed kindness. With the drugs metabolizing in his system, he wasn't so bad. Maybe I could encourage these guys to seek some sort of rehab program. Maybe they came from drug-using families and lacked a real support system. They were probably abused in their own homes, making their own abusive tendencies come out, especially with drug use. I'd read that abuse is a cycle, repeating itself for generations in some families. Child Psychology was an extensive part of my schooling. Although I never dealt with drug families with any of my students, I retained the knowledge from my education.

I realized I genuinely felt bad for these boys. For their upbringing and hard lives. But as soon as I realized how I was feeling, two words popped into my mind: Stockholm Syndrome. Was I really feeling sorry for our terrorizers? I guess I was just trying to make sense of all of it. How not just one, but two people could be so rotten. So callous.

I realized it had been two hours. We'd been going through this hell for two hours. It was almost over. He said so himself. They wanted to be gone by daylight. During this time of year, it would be daylight a little after 6 a.m. Two more hours to go—all of this again? That thought was terrifying.

Surely, they won't wait until the last minute of darkness to leave. That would be too risky. By the time they would exit the gate and make their way down the road, it will be bright outside. People will be out walking and driving around, starting their days. Connor and Jason's faces will be seen. Even if they got away today, with witnesses in town to see their faces, they would end up on the news. No, they wouldn't risk it, I convinced myself. It had to be almost over.

"Jerry, honey. Hold on, my love. We will be okay." I whispered the words. I didn't know why. With Jason standing right next to me, I knew he could hear me.

"I'm alright, Cheryl. My knee hurts more than my pride at this point." The gurgling sound was gone from Jerry's voice. That meant the bleeding from his nose must have stopped, or at least slowed. Good. Another thing I could be thankful for at this point. *We will heal. We will have each other, and we will get a damn security system.*

Jason checked his watch again and groaned. He was getting anxious to get out of here.

"Sit tight," Jason told me, his voice still kind as he walked to the door. He leaned into the hallway. "Connor, what the fuck are you doing, eating leftover meatloaf? Hurry the fuck up."

Connor emerged from the hallway. "As a matter of fact I was. And I went into the garage looking for a pop or something and found an ice pack. I also got a couple of other goodies too." He smirked while patting his pants pocket.

"Unbelievable!" Jason threw his hands in the air and rolled his eyes. "You didn't even bring a pop for me. Selfish prick."

"Whatever man. Go get your own." Connor pushed past him and walked to Jerry. He looked down at Jerry's knee, "Oh shit! My bad, old man, I didn't think I hit you that hard. Sometimes I just lose it and don't realize what I'm doing. Here, this should help a little." He softly set the ice pack down on Jerry's knee.

"Ow!" Jerry screamed, then started panting that heavy breath of intense pain. The same panting I remembered doing after the time I slammed my finger in the car door.

"Thank you, Connor. Thank you for getting the ice pack," I said.

"Sure, lady. Whatever," he said without a care in the world. Not as kind as Jason. Not kind at all. Jason was probably the more mature one. I felt like I was really starting to figure these guys out.

8

CONNOR BENT DOWN TOWARD JERRY, where the ice pack was resting on his knee. Since being hit in the leg, Jerry hadn't been talking much. I imagined the pain must have been so severe that he was just trying not to pass out.

"Old guy, do you wear glasses?"

Jerry looked up at him and seemed confused by the question, as was I. "Um, yeah. Bifocals."

"Where are they?"

Jerry nodded his head over his right shoulder. "Over there on the nightstand. Can you loosen my hands a little bit? My arms are starting to go numb."

Neither of them responded.

"What do you need his glasses for?" I was curious.

Connor grabbed the glasses and put them on Jerry's face. And without turning to look at me, he responded, "Because he's going to need to see this."

Before I could raise my head, Jason grabbed a wad of my hair—again. That same tight grip that had put my scalp in agony just moments ago. This time, he used the grasp to push my face into the carpet. Into my own pile of vomit. It had dried a little by this point, but all the contents from last night's meatloaf were spread from the closet to the floor in front of me, and it was too thick to dry completely.

He moved my head from side to side, making sure my entire face was submerged in the foul chunks and odor. I had both hands on the floor next to my face, trying to push up. I was desperate to escape the stench and suffocation that was quickly overwhelming me. But of course, I wasn't strong enough to do so.

Once he was satisfied that my face was coated, he pulled my aching head up by yanking my hair. I could hear the tearing at the roots this time. Jason told Connor, "Help me move her over, away from this nasty shit. I don't want this on me, it's going to make me gag."

Jerry was hollering, "Stop it! Stop! Leave her alone and deal with me!" I could hear the desperation in his pleas. "I'm the one you want. She has nothing to do with you, or the case. It's not her fault."

Connor, following Jason's command, tried to lift me from the floor. "I'm going to throw my back out trying to move this bitch. She can move herself." He was talking to Jason, but I started crawling anyway. I was on all fours, with dried pieces of last night's dinner clumped on my face. What had just happened? How had I gotten this so wrong?

Even if I was wrong about the drugs wearing off, what about the time? Jason had just been anxiously looking at his watch five minutes ago while waiting for Connor. I didn't understand. And that's what I said.

"I don't understand. You got him ice for his knee and Jason—you're kind. Whatever drugs you're on, you can quit. There's help out there."

"Bitch, what the fuck are you even saying? We don't do drugs," Connor said. "I haven't done drugs since I was twelve. I think much clearer now." They both cracked up laughing.

I felt ridiculous.

"I've never done drugs. I don't even drink, just not my thing. I like to do things with a clear head," Jason chimed in.

Once I was in the middle of the room, Jason pulled out a pocketknife and kissed the silver blade, his eyes fiercely fixated on me. "This won't take long. But make sure to keep your eyes open."

I looked to Jerry helplessly. "I love you." My throat was dry, and my voice cracked. I tried to swallow, but I didn't have any spit.

I anticipated the knife stabbing through me and calmly closed my eyes, defying the order. Instead, I felt a tug at my nightgown. I opened my eyes to see Jason cut the red and white floral pattern straight up the middle. Once he got to the material near my throat, he slowed down. The tip of the blade paused, like he was deciding if he should just shove it into my trachea or not.

He leaned his face close to mine as he made the final cut to the remaining threads. My throat was spared.

"You smell disgusting," he said, and then spit in my face. A loogie landed right between my eyes, then fell to the bridge of my nose. I was mortified. I squeezed my eyes shut as tightly as I could. I could hear Jerry struggling to free himself from the tether.

My nightgown fell open, and I could feel my breasts exposed. The one night I wished I'd worn a bra to bed. I felt warm hands touching each breast. I could feel that one hand was rough and callused, the other soft and much smaller. Two different hands meant two different people. Connor was touching me too.

No. No. No. This isn't happening.

"Please don't," I begged, even though it was already happening.

The hands came off me and I opened my eyes. Connor stood up. It was his rough hand that had been on my right breast. I immediately reached for the sides of my cut gown and attempted to close them. I was so embarrassed and ashamed of my body. I'd stopped changing clothes in front of Jerry a long time ago. When we had sex, I always made sure to keep the lights off. Jerry always told me I was beautiful, but I was self-conscious of the flab that hung, resting in my lap whenever I sat down. I'd been aware of it for years and just never did anything about it. Now these bastards saw it too.

Connor pulled 550 cord from his pocket and walked behind me. He reached around and grabbed my wrists. I had my hands clenched on my gown, holding it together, and didn't want to let it go. He pulled harder and quietly whispered in my ear, "Let it go."

I did.

As he tied my hands behind my back, I put my knees to my elbows in another attempt at modesty. Jason looked at Jerry, who was thrashing so hard to be freed his glasses had fallen onto his lap. Jason went over, picked them up, and cleaned Jerry's sweat from the lenses before putting them back onto his face. "We told you, you have to watch."

"Leave her alone. Take me. Kill me. Just leave Cheryl alone."

"No, sir. You have to watch."

Jerry shrilled at the top of his lungs. An awful scream from the core of his gut. He was breaking down, and it was obvious Jason took pleasure in it by the way he erupted in sardonic laughter.

"This dude is really worried about how much she's going to like this. He probably hasn't been hittin' it right for years. If his dick even still works."

Connor pulled out a roll of duct tape from his other cargo pocket. He tore off a long piece and walked over to Jerry. Jerry seemed to know what was coming, because he turned his head frantically back and forth in an attempt to avoid it. But his efforts weren't enough. Connor stuck the tape over his mouth and slapped it in place. The slap was unnecessary—clearly, it was Connor just finding any way to abuse.

Jason closed the curtains. Either to prevent the upcoming sun from shining through or to prevent anyone from seeing inside. Maybe both. They had no plans of leaving anytime soon. I was abnormally calm given the situation. All I knew was that I wanted Jerry and me to live through this night.

Connor and Jason both stood over me. I closed my eyes, trying not to think of the pain that was inevitably coming. Connor grabbed hold of both my ankles and yanked them, causing my planted feet to give from the floor. My legs were now straight out in front of me, and my gown would not hold without the pressure of my knees against it. With my breasts exposed again, Connor looked up at me and asked, "Are those supposed to be sitting on your stomach?" I didn't answer. I knew it was a rhetorical question. I looked down at my large, naturally sagging breasts, which were hanging to my midsection. I closed my eyes and felt the warmth of a single tear run down my face.

If the fucking humiliation would stop, that would be great.

I didn't say it out loud. That would have only brought on more insults.

Before I even had time to imagine what was coming next, Jason kicked me in the face. The bottom of his heavy boot landed directly against my nose, snapping my head back. I was knocked over, the back of my head smacking the floor. I felt a pop in my right wrist. With my hands tied behind my back, it had snapped between the force of my body weight and the floor. I wiggled my fingers and rotated my wrist. It wasn't broken, but I must have torn a ligament or something.

I didn't lose consciousness, but I began to wish I had. I lay there with my face throbbing. Licking my teeth, I found, luckily, that they were all still in place, but the top two in front had pierced the inside of my upper lip. Unlike my body, I had always taken good care of my teeth. Going to the dentist right on schedule every six months, flossing daily, brushing at least two times a day, and using weekly whitening strips. I frequently get compliments on my smile. It was the only part of my body I was proud of, so I was happy to still have them.

I didn't try to sit back up. I wasn't going to risk another kick to the face. Surely, my teeth wouldn't hold against a second impact. Not wanting to swallow blood, I spit it on the floor. The carpet had already been stained and destroyed anyway.

One of the guys rolled me over onto my stomach. I didn't open my eyes to see which of them it was—it didn't really matter. Once on my belly with my hands tied, I arched my lower back, trying to keep my head up. This position hurt, and my body was quivering at the struggle to maintain the backbend. Connor must have noticed, because he told me, "Use your face as a pillow."

I wasn't comprehending what he was telling me to do. I hesitated, and he said it again, but a lot more pissed off this time.

"Use. Your. Face. As. A. Fucking. Pillow."

I released the hold and put my face directly into the carpet. Slowly, I realized what was coming.

Rape. The word came to me, but I couldn't grasp its inevitable reality. By now I knew Connor was a rapist. He had done it to Jenny. But this just didn't happen in Nashua, New Hampshire, or to people who looked like me. Guys want the pretty women. The ones who make the effort to go to yoga and drink smoothies. The women who use wrinkle cream and who make sure they wash their make-up off each night before going to bed. I didn't do any of those things.

Jerry and I hadn't even made love in months. Gosh, it'd probably been what ... six, no, eight months? I didn't even know. It wasn't because we didn't love each other; we loved each other dearly. When you get to be our age, sex just gets pushed down the to-do list. Plus, Jerry had that month where he couldn't get an erection. The doctors had said it was normal for his age, but Jerry was still embarrassed. He'd tried medication, Viagra, but hadn't kept at it for long. "Real men don't need pills to have sex with their wives," as he said.

He was a prideful man. Usually that was a good thing, a strong thing. But that pride left me on my own for that month. Then the next month he was tired, or I was tired. The month or months following that ... schedules, maybe. Or it'd just been so long that not making love was the new normal. I did remember one time when I got out of the shower, and Jerry pulled my towel open. I screamed at him and smacked his hand away. He looked at me with utter humiliation, then walked out of the room. It wasn't that I didn't want him; oh, I did. But when the towel was open, I felt so ashamed of my body. Disgusted with myself. I hadn't always looked this way. When

I met Jerry, I was at a decent weight. One that fit my frame. That was who he fell in love with. Not this "fat bitch" people saw me as now.

I knew he loved me; I'd never questioned that. It was my own insecurities that held me back.

I hadn't given myself to my husband in months, but here I was, about to be *taken* by these boys. I heard Jerry attempting to yell through the duct tape. I wanted to tell him I was okay, that I'd be okay. But I wasn't. I was numb by this point. I had no fight. Hell, I'd never been a fighter. Never had to be. My father was a strong man, a protector. My grandfather was also a strong man, with an even stronger personality. And not in a good way, not always. He never hurt or abused me, but he became scary when he was angry or drunk. But this … this was about to be my worst nightmare, and there was nothing I could do to stop it.

My mind was spinning. *Think happy thoughts. Think of the kids. Think of anything else but this.*

I was snapped out of my attempts when Jerry started kicking and thrashing against his restraints. He knew what was coming for me too. He was going to have to watch it. They were making sure of that.

If I became violated, would he see me as used goods? Would he still love me? Would he ever want to make love to me again? Even if he wanted to, would he be *able* to? After another man's hands were on my skin. Entering me—and his body sweating on me. As my mind raced with those thoughts, I looked at Jerry fighting so hard to free himself—for me. He was practically pulling his shoulders from their sockets with each jerking movement.

It was then I realized he would always love me. Violated goods or not. His biggest worry would be me. If having sex would hurt me or trigger me back to this detestable night. I knew that to be fact, because his concern was always for me.

Jason was clearly annoyed at Jerry's attempt to free himself. He asked Connor, "Do we have some nails or something to keep this dude in place?"

Nails? Was this kid serious?

Jason was serious. "You know, nails for his eyelids. Ever seen the movie *A Clockwork Orange*? They propped that guy's eyes open with some metal thing and made him watch some fucked-up shit. That's what this fool needs. You wanted him to watch, right?"

A Clockwork Orange. One night, when my kids were teenagers, I walked into the room while they were watching that movie. I looked at the screen and saw a man strapped to a metal chair with a contraption forcing his eyes open. Men standing around him, forcing him to watch some horrific things. I didn't know why they were doing these things to that man, but I knew it was disturbing, and yelled at the kids to turn it off.

Aww, Mom.

That was what they'd say. Mean mom, not wanting her kids to watch ultra-violence. And now these boys were going to do it to us. To my Jerry. They were showing us what they were capable of, and it didn't feel real. It felt like it was out of a movie.

Maybe that was the point.

"Nails won't prop his eyes open, you idiot. He will watch. He's going to want to know what's happening with his ol' lady over here."

I felt one of them grab both my ankles and yank me backward. I wasn't expecting it, so I didn't lift my head from the carpet. My nose and chin burned as the friction of the carpet slid across my skin. I felt the back of my nightgown being pulled up above my butt. I had panties on, not cute ones. They don't really make cute underwear in my size. Or maybe it's that I just don't look for them in the department stores. I wore the cute ones when I was younger and thinner. Nowadays it was all about comfort. I thought for sure these boys would comment on my granny panties, but they didn't.

I propped my face up, using my chin as a platform. I looked across the room at floor level. I was trying to find something to look at, a focal point while this was going to happen. That was when I saw a small black button lying at the base of the dresser. Must have come loose from one of Jerry's shirts at some point in time. I stared at that button so hard. While I focused, Jerry's yells of desperation started to fade. The screams through his closed mouth sounded distant now. I couldn't change what was about to happen, I just wanted to survive it. I felt a tear roll down my cheek, but I wasn't crying. I was trying to focus on something else, so intently that I wasn't blinking. I squeezed my eyes shut for a few seconds to relieve the strain. Then back open—back to the button.

I felt my underwear sliding down my legs. The seams rubbing against my freshly shaved thighs. That was one thing I still did religiously—shave my arm pits, legs, and lady parts. One less thing to be embarrassed about, thank God. I didn't turn around to see who it was. Presumably it was Connor. After all, he was known to be capable of rape. But I hated them both by now. I'd never hated anyone in my life. But I could safely say that at this point, it was all I felt.

After my underwear passed my ankles, I clenched my teeth with fearful anticipation.

Please wear a condom.

As I lay there on my belly, waiting for every woman's worst nightmare to become my reality, I squeezed my thighs together as hard as I could. I fully expected Jason, or more likely Connor, to kick my legs apart. But it was the only defense I had, and I was going to try.

Just as expected, I felt the full weight of a body on my back. It was hard to breathe, and as I lost focus on the button, I heard Jerry stomping his foot on the floor. Presumably from his good leg. I heard his sobs and his muffled pleas. I guess this would be anyone's worst nightmare, if you weren't a monster like these men.

Surprisingly, I discovered the body on my back was Jason when I heard his voice in my ear. "Spread your legs." It was a long, drawn-out whisper. I felt his hot breath on my face and in my ear. I didn't move and I didn't say a word. I tried to find my button. Jerry's thrashing about was making me feel just as helpless.

The next time, he wasn't so kind with his directive.

He put his mouth over my ear and screamed so hard I felt my eardrum rattle, "Spread you goddam legs!"

I didn't do it. I couldn't. I wasn't a fighter, but I also didn't have it in me to give up so easily. I lay there in passive resistance. I fully expected him to use any force possible, which wouldn't take much against my attempt at preventative squeezing. Instead, after a moment, Jason used both hands on my back to push himself up. His push-up caused me to abruptly exhale all my air. My shoulders were aching, and my hands were going numb from being tied up for so long.

So long. Time meant nothing anymore. I'd thought the upcoming sunlight, the dawn of day, would be our savior. But there was nothing and no one coming to our rescue. We didn't have people over in the mornings. Work, maybe? Jerry's boss would notice when he didn't show up. Jerry never just didn't show up. He was never late and had only called in sick one time in the past two years. Surely his boss and co-workers would notice when his desk remained empty after eight o'clock. Same for me. It was my day to work, and someone would have to do something about a classroom full of students without a teacher. But that was a long time from now. So much more could happen. I doubted Jerry was thinking about work right now.

Connor saw Jason's frustration at my non-compliance. "Want me to spread those cankles for you, bro?" He chuckled. "I can tell you've never done this before. Move, you can learn from the master."

"Forget it. I don't think I could get my dick past that fat pork-rind ass anyway."

His comment would have stung an hour before. Now, I barely registered it.

"Come on, man. Fuck her like I did that Jenny Wilson bitch. You'll be a story on the news and be Insta-famous, dude!" Connor burst out laughing.

The boys were joking about rape and how it could make them famous on social media, and it was disgusting.

"Man, shut up."

Jerry blew out wind and inhaled deeply through his nose. I looked at him out of the corner of my eye and released the squeeze I'd somehow been able to maintain. He was pouring with sweat. His soaked hair clung to his forehead and over his ears. He needed a haircut. I'd told him weeks ago, but he'd never made it to the barbershop. Always making excuses. "Long day at work, Cheryl." Or, "It's too packed on weekends with all those new hipster people getting their stupid mustaches waxed." Jerry hated the new trend of young men in their twenties pretending they were from another time. From an era they more than likely knew nothing about.

He looked tired. He was battered and broken, defeat scrawled across his face. It broke my heart. Even though he was relatively "safe" in his secured position, I was more worried about him than I was about myself. Because in my mind, I knew I would be okay. I wasn't so sure about Jerry. I knew he could survive any attack against himself, but would he ever forgive himself for not being able to stop the unimaginable happening to me? That was my concern. Our lives were already changed forever.

9

JASON, BEING THE ANOMALY THAT HE WAS, pulled down a piece of the sheet from our bed and used it to wipe the sweat from Jerry's face. About two feet away from Jerry's leg lay the ice pack from his knee. Jason picked it up and squeezed it just a little. He examined it. Probably to see if it was still frozen. It must have had some coldness left to it, because he set it back on Jerry's knee. My husband was panting with agony and anger.

"You need to stop kicking, so the ice can do its job. That knee is the size of my head, and you're only making it worse."

Jerry grunted and glared up at him. I couldn't see his knee from my faceplant position, but if what Connor said was true, Jerry needed a hospital sooner rather than later. So, I gave it a shot.

"Um, boys ... ahem, fellas. I would really like for my husband to see a doctor. I understand that letting us both go right now would be a risk to you, but what if you let Jerry go to the hospital on his own? If I stayed here with you two, he wouldn't dare say anything to anyone about what has happened. He would never risk the chance of you killing me. So, if you could just let him go or call an ambulance, he could tell them that he fell down the stairs or something."

There was a quiet in the room that told me they were considering it. Until that quiet was interrupted by hysterical laughter.

"Is this bitch for real?" Connor snorted.

Even though the question was a rhetorical one, Jason decided to respond, "I think she's dead-ass serious, dude."

"I came here because of him. He's on the hunt, and it's obvious he wasn't going to stop until he found me. So no, he does not get to leave."

"You're not making the decisions here, lady," Jason chimed in. He leaned into my face. We were nose to nose. His teeth were clenched, and his jaw protruded with each word. "And I'm sick of you talking. So shut your fucking mouth before I cut out your tongue."

I was humiliated at my suggestion and his words sent chills through my spine. My body quivered and I gulped down breaths to stay quiet. I put my face back into the carpet. At least darkness made sense. Burying my face, of my own accord this time, I cried softly. I didn't want them to see it. I couldn't focus on the stupid button anymore. That was a joke, to think staring at a button on the floor would take this nightmare away.

Jerry's heavy breathing wasn't subsiding. He was

getting to the point of hyperventilation. I think we all noticed it at the same time, because Jason told Connor to take the tape from Jerry's mouth.

Connor ripped the tape off, and Jerry gasped frantically for air.

"What's wrong with you, old man? Stop breathing like that!" Connor sounded scared.

Jerry licked his lips and gasped.

I turned to lie on my right cheek, looking at Jerry, who seemed to be having a panic attack.

"Jerry, baby. It's okay. We are okay. Take some slow, deep breaths. Close your eyes and take deep breaths."

Jerry didn't have asthma, and I'd never known him to have a panic attack. But I'd had students in my classroom have panic attacks now and again, so I recognized the symptoms.

Connor went into the bathroom down the hall and brought back a cup of water. I immediately recognized the pint glass with the Steelers logo. Jerry's favorite cup. His lucky cup. Every game night during football season, he drank his beer from it. Connor had probably brought it up earlier after eating our meatloaf.

He poured a small amount into Jerry's mouth, then pulled the cup away. Jerry, being as parched as he was, gulped it down. Connor then poured a tiny bit more. Not even enough for Jerry to swallow. Having the little tease of water with that insatiable thirst clearly irritated him. He spoke through the gasps, "Give me all of it. I've been here suffocating under this tape forever; the least you can do is let me drink that whole cup." When there was no response, he softened his attempt. "I would really appreciate if I could have some more of that water. Please."

"For sure, man." He threw the water into Jerry's face, then dropped the cup onto his lap. All Jerry could do was hang his head while the precious liquid dripped from his face to his shirt, wasted.

"Fuck that guy, come help me sit her up," Jason said, now calling the shots.

Our tormentors knelt next to me. Jason leaned over me and grabbed my left shoulder, rolling me back toward him.

Connor did the same maneuver with my left knee. As I flopped over onto my right side, I was able to look at Jerry directly. He never looked up at me, at least not in the few seconds I faced him. They rolled me onto my back, then sat me upright. My underwear dangled from one foot, and my nightgown maintained its open position. There was no movement I could possibly make to cover my exposed vagina. I focused on what I could do, which was shake my underwear off my friggin' foot. Staring at them down there furthered the humiliation I was already enduring.

I raised my foot and shook it a couple times. They caught my toes and hung there. One more shake—which was more like a kick—and they flew off. I felt like this one decision tonight was mine. An exceedingly small one, but *mine*. This minuscule victory didn't last long before Jason's voice broke in.

"Get on your knees," he instructed me, while

using the back of his hand to wipe sweat from his forehead. Probably sweating from *all* that exertion of rolling me over. I heard the words, but I didn't really get what he was saying. "I'm really sick of telling you shit twice. Get the fuck up."

Because my hands were behind me and my legs lacked the muscle needed to get up, I told him I needed my hands. They had lost all feeling by this point. The 550 cord was way too tight. Much tighter than what was necessary to keep me secured. I wiggled my fingers, hoping some blood would circulate. It felt like a million pins were sticking me, but I had no true feeling. "If you could untie me, I can push myself up."

I was shocked when Connor cut the cord from my wrists. Neither of my captors said a word—he just took out his folding pocketknife and freed me. My shoulders ached when I was finally able to put my arms in front of me. I slowly moved my fingers in agony. The numbness made them feel as if they were a foreign part of me. As soon as the first sign of feeling came back, I didn't *get on my knees* as directed, I reached for my nightgown and pulled it over me. Fragments of dried vomit crumbled down my chin. I looked straight down, not wanting to make eye contact with the guys. I guess I thought if by some chance they weren't looking, I didn't want to look up and draw their attention. I wanted so badly to get this nightgown folded over me, I moved at a slow, methodical pace while I prayed.

Dear Lord, please let this night end. Please just make these guys leave our home. I'm begging you.

Not paying attention. Pfft. What was I thinking? They were standing directly over me. "You know we can see you, right?" Jason asked. He clearly didn't need an answer, but he also didn't stop me. "Now. Get on your knees. If I have to tell you again, Connor is going to have some more fun at your husband's expense."

As I rolled to one side in order to use my hand to push myself up, Jerry spoke up.

"Can you guys just please let my wife get dressed? Put a bra on? Please, allow her to maintain her modesty."

"No one is looking at your wife's tits. I can't even decipher where her tits end and her stomach begins." Connor laughed.

Finally, on my knees, I gave one last tug on my nightgown, ensuring my lady parts weren't exposed. I was feeling more shielded, and I took a long deep breath in, then let it out. I closed my eyes and did it one more time.

"Oh good, she knows how to breathe through her nose. That's about to come in handy."

10

Even being a naive dolt, I knew what Jason meant by that comment. As he grabbed the back of my head, I urinated on myself. Somehow, I was more scared at this point than I was when he took my underwear off. I guess when he was lying on my back, I knew deep down he wasn't going to be able to penetrate me. Somewhat due to my intense thigh squeeze, but mostly because I knew I was too big. Jerry and I had had issues during sex for that very reason. But now … this was definitely going to be possible. It was going to happen.

He pushed my face to his crotch, but his pants were still zipped up. With my face over his clothed groin, I felt his erection growing against my cheek. I had turned my head to the side to avoid my mouth touching the bulge.

Jerry started once again thrashing about, fighting as well as he could. "You piece of shit. Untie me so I can kill you with my bare hands!" He loved me so. Although his adjures were ignored, he continued with maximum effort.

As my knees kept me posted up in my pooling urine, I thought to myself, *why is Jerry the only one fighting here? He's the one tied up, yet he's the one trying to fight for me—for us.* I realized how much of a true coward I had been. I had continued to make excuses all night for not fighting back. I thought being passive and giving them what they wanted would make them stop. I thought being submissive would keep us alive. *Wrong, wrong, and wrong again. It only gets worse. And after all of this, I know they aren't going to let us live. It has got to be morning by now, and they don't have a care in the world.* They didn't know us—our routine. Or who may come by each morning, who was expecting us to call, or text, or show up. They didn't know, and they didn't care.

That was how I knew, finally, that they planned to kill us like they did our poor Shadow. They had been playing games. Games of torture and confusion. Being "nice," then being cruel. Somewhere in the night, I'd forgotten that they were monsters committing egregious acts.

As these thoughts rapidly crossed my mind, I came up with a plan. I couldn't die—or allow Jerry to die—without any attempt to save us. I was going to save us or die trying.

Jerry didn't know my thoughts or my plan, so he was still attempting to free himself. I wanted to say, *Don't worry, babe. I got this.* But I wanted these bastards to think I was going to remain a cowardly fool, so I didn't say a thing. I had prayed. I had God on my side.

Jason grabbed the back of my hair—his favorite

form of physical torture, it seemed—and whispered, "Don't look at me. I know you're a dumb bitch who needs to hear things over and over, so I'll say it again. Do not look at me. I don't want to see your old face while you're sucking my dick." I squeezed my eyes shut and cried. There seemed to be a lot of that happening tonight—today. Whatever time it was now.

Connor reminded Jerry, "The opposite goes for you, old man. You *will* watch. And the second you try to look away, I will carve your eyes out, one at a time. Then you'll wish you could see anything at all." He yanked Jerry's hair—the same way Jason liked to pull mine—and pulled his head up. I wanted so badly to look at Jerry and tell him I loved him, but I couldn't bring myself to look my dear husband in the eye just before performing a sexual act on another man. On a stranger, a monster, in our bedroom.

Jason let go of my head for a second while he unzipped his pants. I kept my eyes closed as instructed, and my body shivered at the sound of the metal zipper going down. I kept my hands hanging by my sides. I got nauseous at the thought of touching him on my own accord. Plus, I wasn't going to need my hands.

Or so I thought.

"Take it out." His voice wasn't a whisper this time. He was making sure Jerry not only watched, but heard as well.

I didn't want him to have to tell me again. I kept my eyes closed—I didn't want to see it. I reached up and felt the gap where the zipper was. The metal prongs that just held him inside his pants were cold against my skin. He was wearing boxer shorts, so I had to move things around to find the opening. His erection had subsided, and its warm softness hung to his left. I was disgusted and mortified. Jerry was yelling and I was shaking so badly I let go of his penis. Without being told again (*I'm finally learning*, I told myself), I grabbed it and put it to my mouth. I touched my pursed lips to the tip of his penis as I maintained a loose hold.

Time for action.

Tightness gripped my chest as I tried to steady by fluttering hands. I had never been an actress, never even done any school plays when I was younger. But right now, I tried to convince my mind that I was playing a role. Telling myself this was not *me* doing this. I went from a two-finger grip to a full hold. I squeezed. Not hard enough to hurt him or make him angry; simply hard enough to get him aroused. It must have worked, because I heard him let out a slight moan. With my eyes still closed, I took him into my mouth. I caressed his penis with my tongue. It didn't take long before he was fully erect. I felt him grow larger inside of my mouth. Larger than he was when limp but he was by no means hung. Below average at best. *Maybe that's why he's a rapist*, I thought, *to make up for what he's lacking.*

I heard Jerry's sobs from beside me. He was doing as he was told; he was watching. It broke my heart hearing his devastation. But I was about to make him proud. I hoped so, anyway.

As soon as I felt the man grow, I followed through with my plan. I took a breath in through my nose, not knowing what was going to happen afterward. But I told myself I was no longer a coward. With my newfound courage, I bit down as hard as I possibly could. I knew I was only going to get one chance. If I bit it off, so be it; he was trying to rape me. He'd forced my face here, and now he was going to pay the consequences.

Jason screamed like a woman in labor and punched me in the side of the head. The solid connect landed directly on my left ear. I only released the bite when I was knocked unconscious.

There was just the hit, then waking up and seeing white spots of light floating all around. My head throbbed so much it made my eyes hurt. It took me a second to focus. I saw a pair of legs stretched out in front of me. Jerry. Shit. I hope they didn't punish him for my action. I rolled my eyes under my lids so I could focus. As the bright floating spots in my vision faded, I realized they weren't Jerry's legs at all. These legs had pants on. *Jason.*

I quickly sat up and heard Jason wincing and taking in frequent short breaths, like he was struggling to get air. I turned and looked around the room, but didn't see Connor

Jerry's voice called out, "Cheryl! Are you okay?"

Was I okay? I was feeling slow and a little confused. I finally told him, "I'm okay, honey. Just gonna have a little bump, that's all."

"You bitch, you fucking bitch," Jason uttered between gasps.

He rolled from side to side with his hands

clutched over his maimed member. I couldn't risk him getting up. My eyes shifted around the room, scanning for anything I could use to keep him at bay. My collection of Precious Moments figurines wasn't going to do much in the way of causing injury.

"I'm going to kill you, bitch." Jason's words were more audible. He was shifting his weight and trying to get up. I couldn't let that happen.

I shuffled past Jason's feet to the nightstand. I picked up the old metal lamp, raising it high above my head. Swinging it down with as much force as possible, I smacked him right in the temple. His body succumbed to the blunt trauma. He was out cold. For a second, I was afraid I'd killed him until I saw the slight rise and fall of his chest. He was breathing.

"Good job, honey! Untie me. We don't have much time."

I crawled to the foot of the bedpost where Jerry was being held. I tried to use my fingernails to work the tight knot, but it wasn't working. I wasn't much of a "do your nails" type of lady. They broke off most times from my calcium deficiency, so they stayed quite short. And they most definitely weren't going to loosen what Connor had accomplished with this cord.

"Shit. It's too tight." My heart was beating fast, knowing I didn't have much time.

Jerry told me to go down the hall to the bathroom and look for nail clippers or anything that could loosen the knot or cut the cord.

Go to the bathroom? I hadn't been allowed to leave my bedroom for hours, and I was now almost scared to. Plus, Connor was still somewhere in the house. I turned and stared at the open door. I stopped messing with the knot and just stared into the hallway, listening. I didn't hear any movement outside of the room. All I could hear were Jason's moans.

Who's the bitch now?

I was proud of my work. I would never have spoken that way to people, but the thought of it made me feel a little more empowered.

"Honey, where did the other one go? Did you hear the front door at all?"

"I don't know. When you fucked up this guy ..."

"Babe!"

Jerry never talked that way either. Maybe at work, but never around me.

"Well, it's what you did! And I'm proud of you for it. Anyway, after you *took down* Jason, Connor's face turned white as a ghost and he ran out. Shit, my face probably went transparent. As any man's in the room would have." He gave a sick, sad laugh. "But I don't know where he went when he left the room."

It was good to hear him laugh, even if only for a second.

I went to the doorway but didn't cross the threshold into the hall just yet. I wanted to hear if Connor was coming back. If he was, he was going to unleash holy hell on us. If he was able to do all those horrible things to Jenny and just dump her poor body out in the elements to rot, he wouldn't have a problem doing the same, or worse, to Jerry, who was actively hunting for him. Jenny hadn't done anything at all. She was a sweet teenager with the rest of her life ahead of her, and Connor didn't care about any of that.

"How long has it been? Since Connor left. How long was I out?" I asked Jerry all at once, frantic, the words tumbling out.

"It's only been a few minutes. You weren't out long. I think once your head hit the floor, you came to a little bit."

Wow. I felt like I'd lost a few hours. My head was still aching. *Focus.*

No movement was coming from the bathroom down the hall. But the bathroom light was off, that much I could tell.

I looked down at Jason's motionless body, then back into the hall. I had no sympathy for him or his unfortunately sized member.

I was terrified to leave my bedroom, which I now, ironically, felt most safe in.

"Hurry up, Cheryl. We don't have much time; you have to go. You had the courage to fight back just a little while ago, you have to keep going."

He was right. I'd had one little success in a full night of hell, and it wasn't over yet. I went into the hallway and tip-toed toward the bathroom. I had memorized where all the loose floorboards were and knew when to side-step to avoid the squeaking sound they made when stepped on directly. I'd had to learn these spots. If I got up in the middle of the night to use the restroom and stepped on a squeaky board, it would always wake up Shadow, who would bark and bark and bark until Jerry woke up too, asking what was going on. I guess it was easier to learn where to step than to just get the floor fixed.

I made it to the bathroom without being detected. I knew Jason was in no condition to yell or alert Connor, and I hadn't heard a peep from anywhere in the house. I bet Connor had wanted to keep his pecker and fled, leaving his friend behind. I'd watched those crime shows on TV. Every time one of the criminals got caught, it was because his friend told on him or because the friend left him behind. That felt like exactly what was happening here. After all, Connor was the leader. The "shot caller" — that was the term they used on that show, *Lock Up*. I think it was why I always thought the type of crimes that were now occurring in my home only happened to other people. Those people on the news, or on true crime shows, separated by the screen. But I was forgetting that those true crime shows were *true*. Real people, who I now could relate to.

I tried to feel around in the dark, but quickly realized that wasn't going to work. It was making too much noise. I needed to turn on the light and look fast. I flipped the switch, and the light flooded out into the hall. My reflection in the mirror cause me to stop dead in my tracks. Dried vomit lay in patches all over my face. Blood had seeped past the corners of my mouth. I looked older somehow. Worn out. My ear was bright red from Jason's blow. My hair was in knots from each time Jason had gripped it in his fist. I realized the blood on my lips was still wet. Not the dried blood from my tooth piercing my lip hours ago.

That was when it hit me—it was Jason's blood. "Ha!" I said out loud, but quietly. I was proud. *That's what he gets.* I didn't even worry about possible STDs or anything at this point. I just hoped I'd rendered that little pecker useless. If I survived this night, I would never forget these bastards; but now, at least one of them wouldn't forget me either.

Now I had to hurry. I doubted Connor was still around, but Jason could wake up and fight off of pure anger and adrenaline. Looking through drawers and under the sink, I realized how much crap we had. Suntan lotions, hair products, shampoos and conditioners Jerry always insisted we buy in bulk. And nothing was what I needed. I started out moving things quietly, but quiet wasn't quick. So, I started just pulling things out and tossing them aside.

Something sharp, something with a cutting edge, anything.

My desperation was making me feel helpless. I wished Jerry were the one in here looking. He would be able to Macgyver something out of all this stuff.

God, just cut me one more break. Just one more.

I opened the medicine cabinet. Expired medications, Band-Aids, ointments, face creams. Then I saw it—a nail file with clippers. Okay, not the best, but it was something. And that was all I'd asked for. "Thank you, Jesus!" I whispered out loud. I'd be sure to let the church ladies know on Sunday how prayer does work. I dissolved into laughter at the thought of telling this—any of this—to the women at church. Oh the looks on their faces. We would come together in prayer after a morning of hymns and give thanks for making it out alive. How blessed Jerry and I would be to even make it to Sunday. Praise the Lord.

But first things first—we still have to make it out alive.

With file in hand, I peeked out of the bathroom door to make sure the coast was clear. I turned off the bathroom light to give my eyes time to adjust to the darkness of the hallway. Then I looked and listened. With no sight or sound of Connor, I made my way back down the hall with my precise steps. I moved a bit quicker going back than I had on my way there.

When I got back to our bedroom, Jerry looked startled but relieved to see me. "Shit, I thought you were Connor. Did you find something?"

I held up the file and clippers and smiled. We were going to get out of here.

Jason was still in the position he'd landed in when I cracked him a good one. I looked closely at his face. He appeared to be in shock. His eyes were open now, but he had that thousand-yard stare. His hands had released their hold on his junk, and his limp, bloody, penis was hanging out from his open zipper. I was still proud.

I sat down beside Jerry and began working the binding. I first tried using the nail clippers. I thought it was going to cut with just a couple snips, but that didn't happen. I was only making very small indents, nothing useful. What was this stuff made of? Working the knot with the file might be a better, faster solution. Dropping the clippers, I picked it up and tried shoving it into the middle of the knot.

"Is it working? Come on Cheryl, hurry."

I was trying. But my hands were shaking, and I could barely feel them because my adrenaline was so high. I was hoping Connor was gone, but Jason was still here. How long shock lasted, I didn't know.

"I'm trying, honey. I'm afraid Jason is going to snap out of it,"

I was able to get the file through the knot, but it was difficult to move it once it was in there. It wasn't helping at all. I tried using the file as a saw, pulling it back and forth inside of the knot.

"Put the file in my hand. I can work through it while you find some sort of weapon in case Connor comes back. Don't worry about Jason right now. That snoring sound he's making isn't because he's asleep. Snoring respirations means you knocked him a good one."

I did what Jerry asked. As he worked to free himself, I went through our drawers and under the bed. Nothing. Then Jerry had a good idea.

"Cheryl, grab a piece of broken wood from the closet door. I don't care how long it is, just grab the piece with the sharpest end."

Good thinking. As I got to the closet, the odor of my vomit was more overpowering than it had been all this time on my face. The pile was still wet. I gagged and covered my mouth. It was this delay that caused me to blow it.

Connor emerged from the hallway without a sound.

"What the fuck are you two doing? No, no, no.

Can't leave you alone for a minute."

I was startled and looked up at him in shock. He was still here. Where had he been? What was he doing? I was about to get my answer.

11

JERRY WAS JUST AS SURPRISED AS I WAS. He looked at his legs outstretched before him and started shaking his head. I could see the defeat in his face, the same defeat I was feeling. I was taking so long to process the fact that Connor had still been here this whole time that I didn't even think about running or fighting.

Then I saw his hands. In his right hand, he held a hammer. One of Jerry's, from our garage. I knew it was Jerry's because it had a red handle, and Jerry had a whole set of those. The head had one round side and one flat side. It wasn't a regular hammer; it had a name that I couldn't quite remember. During the times I sat with Jerry as he worked on things in the garage, I would be his assistant and hand him the tools he needed. I wasn't much interested in tools; it was just my way of spending time with him.

In Connor's other hand, he had some sort of straight metal tool. What was that? With it down by his side I couldn't quite get a good look at it.

"You." Connor used the hammer to point at me.

"Don't move. If I see you reach down for any of that splintered wood, if I see you move at all, I will use this to crush your hands. Do you understand me?"

I nodded.

"Why don't you just leave now?" Jerry asked.

"Please. Your friend is injured and I'm sure he needs to see a doctor." He was trying to reason with him.

"You think I'm just going to walk out after what your fuckin' wife did to him?" He pointed to Jason, who was still on the floor. "You're fucking crazy if you think I'm going to let that shit go. That was some fucked-up shit she did. She didn't have to do that. All he needed was a little head. He hasn't gotten any in a long time—can't blame a dude for just trying to get some. Had he just busted his nut, we could have been outta here. But look at him." Connor pointed at Jason. "He's hurting, bad. And I don't like when people hurt my friends."

Connor leaned in close to look at Jason's motionless body. He appeared confused at Jason's state of duress. "What the fuck did you do to him? You fucking killed him!" His face quickly turned a dark red. Those beautiful amber eyes were full of darkness now as he glared at me with vicious intent. Like pure evil was trying to escape him.

Fear was an understatement—I was petrified. "He's not dead. Listen, he's breathing just fine." I was hoping he didn't know about this bad snoring Jerry had just educated me on. If he was aware, Jerry chimed in before he had time to speak.

"You raped and murdered a girl, and you don't like when people are hurt? You're going to hell for what you did to that girl. No matter what you do to us tonight, you won't get away with what you did to Jenny."

Even through all his pain and all we had been through, Jerry had never lost sight of justice. His mission all along had been to catch Jenny's attacker, and he wasn't giving up on that.

Connor didn't respond. Instead, he took two large steps that landed him directly in front of me. Leaning in close to my face, he said, "You hurt my friend. And now you're going to pay for it." He backed up and walked to Jason's other side, dropping the two tools by his feet. I now had a clear view of the straight metal tool. It was a punch from Jerry's brand new Mayhew Pro tool set.

This can't be happening. What is he planning to punch through?

Connor didn't ask Jason if he was okay; he already knew the answer. It was evident by his condition. He simply told him, "It's going to be okay, man. I got you, I'm gonna handle it." He patted the other man's head as if he were a little boy.

I put my hand on Jerry's leg and rested my head on his shoulder. There was no way to prepare for the unknown of what was about to happen. But I wanted Jerry to know I loved him, and we were going to go out together. 'Til death do us part.

Connor picked up his tools—our tools. Tools he'd clearly spent so much time looking for and deciding on in our garage. Time contemplating and imagining what damage each tool could cause to a human.

He'd settled on these two items. He must have precisely envisioned his plan for each one. I wondered if he'd laughed or smiled when his decision was finalized.

Jerry laid the side of his face on top of my head, acknowledging what was probably going to be our final minutes on this earth.

Connor pulled my arm, trying to stand me up. "Get up." I didn't hesitate. I was so devastated—my victory had come to an end so abruptly. At this point, I almost felt willing to accept our fate. I didn't want to die, but I knew my God was up there, ready to accept me with open arms.

I stood, waiting for further instruction.

"Go to the other side of the bed, and sit on the floor, facing away from me."

I complied. I took my place on the side, but near the foot of the bed, so I could turn and keep Jerry in my sight.

Connor dropped the tools and removed his pocketknife from his pants. He flicked the blade open with one swift motion. Clearly, he was no stranger to knives. Pointing the silver blade at the tip of Jerry's nose, he tapped it just slightly.

"You know what, old man? You think you're so smart. All these years you're looking for me because of that Jenny chick. Trying to fuck up my life. Telling the news there's this guy … this homicidal rapist on the loose. But what about Vanessa? Why didn't you ever go after her?"

I was confused, and looked to Jerry for an answer.

During all the years as the detective assigned to the case, his time as a private investigator re-opening the case, he'd always referred to the perp as a guy. And here he was, in front of us. What was Connor talking about?

Jerry's brow scrunched and his eyes squinted. He seemed just as confused as I was.

Connor started laughing and threw his hands in the air. "You can't be for real, man. You're supposed to be this badass detective, and you never figured out that I didn't do that shit alone?" He laughed and began pacing in circles around our room. "Vanessa is my chick. She went to school and played soccer with your poor Jenny. That is, until that little snitch ratted her out for having a little bit of pot in her locker and got Vanessa expelled. The whole thing was her idea. How the hell did you never figure that out?" He seemed shocked and amused at our lack of insight.

I felt sick, and Jerry's face had turned red. "You're lying. I talked to everyone at that high school and on the soccer team. No one mentioned anyone named Vanessa. None of Jenny's friends or family ever mentioned a friend or former friend with that name. You can't dump your crimes on someone who doesn't exist."

"Wow. You really do suck at your job. I didn't even need to come here tonight, huh; you would have never found me. Fuck. Some tough guy cop you turned out to be." He scoffed. "Dude, let me help you out. You didn't hear about Vanessa because she was expelled at the start of the school year. She's a couple years older. And she wasn't friends with that loser girl. And when she got expelled and found out she couldn't go to college, she asked me to help ruin that girl's life, like she had ruined Vanessa's. The whole plan was hers.

"She went to Jenny's soccer practice that day and told her she wanted to apologize for the names she'd called her when she was escorted off campus. She offered Jenny a ride home so they could talk and make amends. That dumb bitch actually bought that shit. She got into the car, and Vanessa drove her to me where I waited in the park, in the wood line near the waterfront. At first, Vanessa just wanted to rough her up. Cut her face so Jenny wouldn't forget her. But that girl came out with a fury. Vanessa took some kicks trying to drag her out of the car. So, I grabbed her legs and yanked her out. The back of her head caught the doorframe and knocked her silly. You should have seen her, man. Her eyes rolled back like a zombie movie."

He laughed.

"Jerry," I said, "he's lying. He's trying to get a rise out of you. He's trying to take the blame off himself. You worked on this for years, you know this was a solo guy crime. Ignore him."

Jerry's jaw protruded in rhythm as he kept clenching his teeth. But he didn't say anything. Connor just kept talking.

"When she hit the ground, she just lay there. Fuck, I didn't know what to do. But her young legs looked so sexy in those short shorts. Same way Vanessa's turned me on. You know how it is being a man." He winked at Jerry. "I rubbed her thigh a little bit. I didn't

109

think Vanessa was gonna let me do it, but she says, 'Fuck her and let's get out of here.' Shit, if my chick gives me the green light to fuck another chick while she watches, I'm not turning that down. You know what I'm sayin'? These girls these days, they dress in these short shorts and shave their bodies, they want us to come at 'em I know your bitch over there doesn't get it, but you know what I'm sayin', right, man?" He slapped Jerry on the shoulder, like this was some sick bonding moment.

"No, you sick motherfucker, I don't know. She was a child." Jerry's anger was overtaking his pain.

"Well, she was a tight little thing. Definitely a virgin. Always my favorite. Right when I shot my load in her, she woke up and started screaming. She tried to grab at my face, so Vanessa held her arms down until I was done. 'Til I let that last little bit out. Vanessa's a good chick. A ride-or-die. Anyway, that girl wouldn't stop her screaming. The river was close, too many people were gonna hear, so I put my hands around her neck and squeezed. I kept telling her to shut the fuck up, but she wouldn't. Tough little whore. She finally stopped screaming and stopped moving. Vanessa grabbed that girl's bag from the car and tossed it. We took off. That was it. Case solved now. Huh, old man?"

I didn't know whether to believe this Vanessa story or not. Jerry and so many other detectives had worked the case for so long. Maybe that was just one of the many leads the guys had had. Jerry would often tell me when they'd gotten a lead, but wouldn't often mention what it consisted of.

"Where's Vanessa now? If she's so good to you, why didn't you bring her here tonight for your revenge instead of Jason?"

It was a good question.

"I told you, Vanessa's a good chick. Loyal. This is my revenge, not hers. You weren't blasting anything about her on the news or fliers. She's somewhere safe, waiting for me to come back. She's scot-free. But since you started looking for me again, I had to do something. If I ever got caught and locked up, I'd have to worry about all these bros out here trying to get at my girl, and risk another dude raising my kid. I can't have that. Na, man. You gotta be dealt with."

My jaw fell open and I shuddered at the notion of this man having a child. I felt sorry for a kid I didn't know. Because with Connor as a father, that little boy or girl didn't stand a chance in life.

I was disgusted and in disbelief at Connor's words. He was a cold, callous, disturbed human being. He spoke of raping and killing Jenny as if it was just something he and his girlfriend did for fun. Killing Jenny had been Vanessa's revenge, and killing us was going to be his.

"I can't believe I missed it," Jerry said with a blank stare.

"You didn't miss anything, honey. He's probably lying." I was trying to reassure him.

"The necklace. The fucking necklace had female DNA on it. I completely dismissed that evidence and never thought about it again. I figured, of course there's female DNA, because of Jenny."

Connor chimed in, "Oh shit, the Claddagh necklace I gave to Vanessa so she would be reminded of me at all times. I'm American by birth, but Irish by blood. We didn't realize that thing was missing until days later. Should have known that little twat managed to rip it from Vanessa's neck. She loved that necklace; can we get it back? Ha."

The information hit me almost as hard as it clearly had hit Jerry. I remembered those years ago when the lab had called to report the DNA. Female DNA at that. I didn't realize Jerry had dismissed it, assuming it was Jenny's without having tested it.

My body racked with an onslaught of sobs as grief left me in a flood of uncontrollable tears. I couldn't believe I was living this nightmare. I just wished our doorbell had never rung.

12

"CRAWL OVER HERE." I knew Connor was talking to me by process of elimination. Crawl. *Here we go again with the demeaning treatment.* But after what I'd just heard, I knew I shouldn't expect anything less.

I got onto all fours and reached back to pull my cut nightgown down. It wore more like a robe at this point, but I wanted to make sure my butt was covered. For some odd reason, I still felt it was important to make that attempt at humility. These guys had already seen my naked ass —but it didn't matter. I didn't want them to see it again.

I crawled to Connor's feet and sat back on my heels, not daring to stand up without being ordered to do so.

"Good girl." He looked at me, looked back at Jason, then looked at me again. "Sit next to him."

I looked at the man on the floor and cringed at the thought of being that close to him again, but I complied. What choice did I have?

Jerry was twisting side to side as I crawled toward Jason. His movements were awkward. I looked into his beautiful light brown eyes to see if he was in shock from the pain or from all Connor had just unleashed on him. He glanced back at me for a split second, then squeezed his eyes shut. All while still doing the subtle twisting. I chalked it up to his pain and frustration. He was maintaining his composure so well given what his nose and knee looked and probably felt like.

I took my place—so close to Jason it would have taken minimal movement to reach over and touch him. Not that I wanted to. Anxiety hit me fast and hard. My heart was racing, my breaths shallow and frequent. I had a lump in my throat and tried to swallow. My mouth was so dry I couldn't produce any saliva to coat it. I hadn't had water all night, and wasn't dumb enough to ask for any. I hadn't even thought to earlier.

Connor was seemingly satisfied with our positioning. He had a crooked smile on his face, with only the left side of his mouth curling upward. After picking up the tools from the floor, he looked at Jason and told him, "This one's for you."

My eyes were fixated on the tools in his hand. The hammer in one, the punch in the other. He had a tight-fisted grip on them. The veins in his hands were bulging. He kicked my outstretched legs apart and got close to me. His waist was level with my face. *Dear Lord. I don't know what is about to happen, but I know this is going to be the end of us.* I had yet to hug Jerry and give him a proper goodbye. I'd never got the chance to call the kids and tell them they were the loves of my life. *I hope they know.*

I looked down and saw my hands were visibly

trembling. I clenched my fists. Not because I was going to fight back, no—those times were over for me. Because I didn't want Connor to see the shaking. I didn't vomit, and I didn't urinate on myself this time. I felt like Jerry and I had done our best, and my only hope at this point was that my ultimate demise would be quick and painless.

"Look at me, fat bitch."

I peered into Connor's eyes. Dark and demonic. They were soulless, as if his body were the shell for something sinister contained inside. And after hearing the details of what he'd done to Jenny, I wasn't sure there *was* anything inside.

"You really fucked up my friend over there. You bit straight through his dick. It's barely hanging on. So I'm gonna make sure you can never do that to any man, ever again. Now smile."

Time seemed to slow down. All the sounds in the room faded away. I looked at Jason and the blood that had pooled next to him. The walls blurred when I looked around the room and noticed things I hadn't seen or hadn't bothered to acknowledge in a long time. There was a fold of the wallpaper on the top corner near the window. I forgot we still had that wallpaper. I asked Jerry so many times over the years to take it down. It was dated with pink and green flowers. But the longer he put off taking it down, the more I forgot it was there. It sure was god awful.

Above the dresser, I saw the smashed spider that had never been scraped away. I chuckled as I recalled the Valentine's Day when Jerry had insisted on a lavish dinner date. Normally, he wasn't the type to want to get dressed up and go out. But that year, he insisted. I was giddy with excitement as I took a pearl necklace from the jewelry box. I looked up into the mirror and saw something run by and disappear behind the dresser. I screamed for Jerry and he came running in quickly. He looked so silly in his black dress socks, boxer shorts, and fancy white long-sleeve button-down shirt with covered placket and pique plastron. It was a fancy Yves Saint Laurent brand, given to him by our daughter to wear for her wedding. Far too extravagant for someone of Jerry's gruff, but he wore it anyway because it was such a kind gesture and it meant a lot to him.

Just as the little bugger came running back out from behind the mirror, Jerry picked up his slipper and realized he was too short. His attempts at jumping to get to the elusive insect sure gave me a good laugh though. He finally just threw the slipper wildly, and he smashed the thing. I never got close enough to see what kind. Neither of us did. The thrown shoe had stuck it in place high on the wall. We always meant to get a ladder in here and wash it off, but as time went on, it never happened. And here I was, seeing it now. That dead spider was a sign of better times.

I didn't smile as told. But it didn't stop anything. Connor easily slipped the tip of the punch between my lips. I felt the pressure of its sharpness against my gums directly above my front teeth. With the hammer in his other hand, I knew what was coming. Maintaining my gaze on Connor, I thought of the kids. I hoped they were safe and warm in their beds.

My entire body was shaking uncontrollably. My trembling chin and lips were causing the sharp tip to scratch my gums with every movement. I clenched my jaw and squeezed my eyes shut as tight as I could.

Jerry screamed a long, drawn-out, "No! Don't you do it. Focus on me, I'm the one you're here for." He was thrashing about so hard I worried about him breaking his wrists between the cord and the wood of the bedpost.

Connor, of course, ignored him.

When Connor raised the hammer, I felt his grip on the tool tighten. I felt pressure and scraping at my gums, but not pain. Not yet. Tears flowed from the corners of my eyes down my face.

Please God, just let me pass out.

When the first tear dripped from my chin, I was ready. I squeezed my fists, took a deep inhale, and held my breath.

Just as I expected the strike, I heard a loud bellow.

"Ahhhh!" belted deep from Jerry's core, followed by a loud thud. The punch fell from my lips, hitting my knee before landing on the floor.

Jerry had freed himself just in time to save me from the horror I was about to endure. I realized it all at once—that was what his odd twisting and rocking back and forth had been about. He was working that cord.

My husband tackled Connor. They were wrestling around on the floor and Jerry was punching anywhere and everywhere he could. He was grunting and growling and fighting in a way I didn't know

Jerry was still capable of. I was seeing him defend me with everything he had, using all his military and police training from so long ago.

"Cheryl, run! Get out! Go get help, do it now."

At first, I didn't move. Jason was rolling back and forth, trying to get up, but he couldn't. Connor was swinging wildly back at Jerry, but he didn't appear to be landing any hits. And if he was, he wasn't doing any damage. Jerry's adrenaline and anger were allowing him to move without thinking about his knee or his nose. His t-shirt was soaked in sweat and stained with his own blood.

Jerry finally got on top of Connor in a full-mount-type position. I'd been around Jerry and his friends enough while they watched those martial art ring fights, bringing them snacks and beer. They would sometimes cheer and yell out when their fighter was able to get the opponent in the full-mount position. Their excitement had me looking at the screen. I wondered if Jerry had learned that move from watching those fights or if it was something he'd been trained in.

From his position straddling Connor's midsection, he turned to me and said it again. "Run. Get out, now!"

I watched for a brief moment as Jerry struggled to hold on. Connor managed to slip his arms free. Snapping back into focus, I got up and pulled my nightgown closed. Reaching to my feet, I picked up the punch that had been so close to knocking out my teeth. With all their thrashing about, I didn't want to accidentally get Jerry. So I stabbed Connor as hard as

I could in his shin. The punch went deep and stood straight up in place. Connor screamed in pain. Not a fatal wound by any means, but I hoped it helped. Maybe it'd give Jerry an upper hand. Even a little help was help.

I stepped over Jason, who was unable to stop me, and ran along the hall and down the stairs, my bare feet smacking against the old hardwood floor. I made it to the bottom of the stairs, then stopped dead in my tracks.

I gasped in horror and covered my mouth at the sight of Shadow's lifeless, bloody body. "Oh baby, I'm so sorry." I leaned down, gave her a quick pet, and kissed her. I heard loud thuds from the floor above me and realized I was wasting time. I threw the front door open and was blinded by the sunlight. It was morning, but I had no idea what time. There was no one in sight. I screamed out in desperation. The only response was the singing of the morning birds. Squinting and using one hand as a visor, I tried to focus on the guard tower in front of me. It was about a hundred yards straight ahead. Running to a neighbor's house would have been closer, but I needed a man with a gun. Barefoot and in my soiled nightgown, I set out for help.

PART II: JERRY

13

"You come into my house in the middle of the night, torture me and my wife, and you think you're going to walk out of here?"

I didn't care how bad my knee was. I decided then and there that Connor was not going to get away with this. What he and Jason had done to my wife—my Cheryl—they would pay.

Connor rolled me off him. "You're not the tough man you used to be. Look at you. You're old, beaten, and broken. You put up a good fight just now, but the battle isn't over."

We were both exhausted. We sat on the floor trying to catch our breaths and observe our wounds. Connor didn't have a dislocated knee, but I roughed him up somethin' good. He pulled the punch from his leg and threw it across the room.

"Like I told you, I can't have you looking for me. I don't give a fuck about that Jenny girl or her stupid family. That girl should have never fucked with Vanessa. Actions have consequences. People seem to forget that these days. And this is your consequence.

You were getting too close. I have a little girl to raise now, and I can't do it from prison."

"You have a daughter? You having a kid is one thing, but a little girl? What if someone does to her what you and Vanessa did to Jenny? What would you do then? You say actions have consequences, but actions also come with karma. Ever think of that?"

Clearly angry at the thought, Connor stood up with his fists clenched and white-knuckled. Raising one fist to my chin, he addressed me. "Don't you ever wish bad shit on my daughter. You hear me? We're gonna give her a good life. As long as you're not around to ruin it."

He walked over to Jason. "Dude, I'm gonna finish this guy and get the fuck outta here. I can't carry you like this. Plus, you need a hospital and I can't be seen there. I'm sorry, man. Don't say shit about me to the police. Just tell them you wanted to rob a house for some extra cash or something."

As Connor made his plans to leave Jason behind, I thought about my wife. About all she'd been through tonight, and that she was out there alone. What if Connor left here and caught up with her? Cheryl wouldn't be moving too fast. And I'd been waiting to be face-to-face with this guy for so many years. There was no way I was letting him get away.

I crawled across the floor, dragging my bad leg as Connor walked out of the room. I heard the faucet turn on down the hall. He was in our bathroom washing up. He must have known he'd draw too much attention if he walked out looking the way he did. I had to hurry. The police were going to arrive soon, and now that Cheryl was safe, it was time. It was personal now. I had to handle him myself.

Making it to my nightstand, I found the set of keys I needed. Jason knew I was up to something; I saw it on his face. But after what Connor had just said, I doubted he was going to try and alert him. That much, I felt confident about.

I stood up and peered down the hall. The sink was still running. Lucky for me, because that prevented him from hearing me step into the hall on the first creaking floorboard. I'd never learned which ones to avoid like Cheryl did.

I shuffled down the stairs, using the handrail as my crutch. Brightness flooded the house from the front door, which Cheryl had left open. I made it down the stairs faster than I ever had with two good legs. I reached the landing and saw Shadow's little lifeless body.

Motherfuckers.

My anger and sickness at the sight of her propelled me to push on. I made my way past the living room to the hallway closet. Opening the door, I had to stand on the tip-toes of my good leg to get the box I was looking for. My mind was racing through the possibilities of how this was going to end. There was a tightness in my chest, and it was growing with every breath.

I put the metal box on the closet floor and began fumbling with the keys. My fluttering hands were making gripping them almost impossible.

I don't have much time. If I let him leave, he's going to

find Cheryl.

Taking a deep breath, I tried one key at a time. I hadn't bothered to label them. I inserted the first key into the lock, but it wouldn't turn. The second key wouldn't even fit the hole. Then I heard the water stop. I froze for a second to listen. Heavy footsteps led back into our bedroom.

I only have a few seconds before he realizes I'm not there and he makes his way down to me.

The footsteps turned into running almost immediately. The thud of Connor's boots got louder as he made his way down the stairs.

I got it!

The box lid flew open, and there was my beautiful 9mm Smith and Wesson, the one that I'd carried as a duty weapon for so many years. The gun I had pointed at more people than I could count but was fortunate enough to never have to use. Until now.

Connor jumped over Shadow's body without a second look. I pulled back the slide and loaded the bullet into the chamber. Connor heard the distinct sound of the metal clanking, unmistakable to anyone who has ever handled a handgun. And by the look on Connor's face, he knew exactly what it was.

He turned and ran out the door as I advanced with gun in hand.

I can't let him get away with this.

That was the last thought in my mind before my index finger steadily pulled back on the trigger, releasing the lead projectile. I walked out into the sunlight and fired two more follow-up shots. You see, police, military, or anyone properly trained with a firearm aren't taught to fire just one shot. That rarely stops a threat. Three times. That's how we trained, and that's what I did.

After the third shot, I lowered the gun to my side and looked at the holes I'd just put in Connor's back. He lay face down in my yard. The shot group was tight, especially for a moving target. I had never shot anyone before, and I got the tunnel vision that had been described to me so many times by those who had. I couldn't see anything else around me but the surrounding darkness of the temporary loss of vision and the blurry light to my front. Everything went quiet except for the ringing in my ears. No singing of birds in the early hours, no sound of cars in the distance … just high-pitched ringing.

My chest was pounding with the adrenaline pumping through my heart. For the first time in decades, I felt scared and sick to my stomach. I didn't want this.

My vision came back into focus when I finally looked up and saw police cars facing the house. I didn't know how long they'd been there. The red-and-blue lights oscillated around me as officers took cover behind their car doors with guns drawn. Pointed directly at me. I looked back and forth and couldn't figure out why they weren't pointing their guns at Connor. He was down, but he was the threat. He was the bad guy here.

I focused in on one young cop, and the barrel of his black semi-automatic handgun pointed at my chest. He couldn't have been older than twenty-four. He was tall, and his hair was cropped neatly. I wondered if this was the first time he'd had to draw his gun.

The first time is the scariest; I remembered it well. I was working graveyard shift when this young punk who'd just robbed a convenience store at gunpoint ran directly toward me. He had his hand in his jacket pocket and wasn't following my orders to stop. I drew my gun and pointed it at the kid. *Please don't shoot me, kid. Please don't make me shoot you.* My hands could hardly keep steady. The kid, all of sixteen years old, finally complied with my orders. He put his hands up and kneeled on the ground. After I put the cuffs on him, I removed a handgun from his pocket. I checked to see if it was loaded, and found it was a BB gun. I couldn't believe it. *Stupid, stupid kid.* My fear turned into anger at the "what could have happened" scenario.

I was wondering if this young man now standing in front of me was shaking like I had so many decades ago. I locked in on his face. His mouth was moving, but I couldn't hear words. The longer I held his gaze, the more my hearing started to fade back into reality. I heard yelling, but the words were unintelligible. Blinking slowly, I took in the scene in front of me. I had never been on this side of the law before. It was vastly different.

As the officer's voice started to resonate with my slow comprehension, I understood. "Drop the gun or you will be shot!"

Looking down, I saw my white knuckles clutching the gun in my hand. I hadn't even realized I was still holding it. I had trained with and shot guns for most of my life, but now the grip felt foreign in my hand. I feared it. Much like when first-time shooters pick up a gun. The weapon is scary—it feels like it can kill you of its own accord without any human touching it.

With a flick of my wrist, I sent the gun sliding onto the sidewalk in front of me. I followed the young officer's orders to get on the ground with my hands in the air. He had excellent command presence, and his directions were clear and concise. I didn't know him, but I was proud of him. He'd make a fine officer, indeed.

I raised my arms high and dropped to my knees. But with one knee out of commission, I leaned over and put all my weight on my good side. I had been through this scenario so many times in past trainings, but this was different ... the real-life version. My battered body struggled to lower myself to the position into which I was ordered. Surely this was just protocol. I was covered in blood and had a gun in my hand. Plus, this cop didn't know who I was. He didn't know all the years I wore that shiny badge he was proudly displaying on his puffed-out chest. All he knew right then was that I was a bloody man in my boxer shorts who'd just shot another man in my front yard. Cheryl probably told them of two male intruders in our home, and by the looks of me, I could be one of them. Once this young man went through the proper steps he was taught in the academy, I'd have my chance to explain. He would know that I'd just protected my wife and apprehended the suspect who tried to flee.

I maintained the position I wished all the suspects in my past had done. I wanted to make it easier for these guys to do their jobs. No sudden movements and follow instructions. Even doing everything right, being on the other end of that black barrel raised the hair on the back of my neck. The last thing I needed was some nervous newbie getting an itchy trigger finger. But seeing all these cops here told me Cheryl had made it to them. *She must be okay. It's all okay now.*

Two paramedics ran up, pushing a gurney. Neither of them looked at me. They either didn't perceive me as a threat, or they were just working as they were trained. Triage. Treat the most severely injured first. That was Connor, so my feelings weren't hurt when they bypassed my bloody face and mangled knee.

I thought of Jason and how Connor had left his friend, whom he'd dragged into this. Don't get me wrong, I didn't feel bad for him by any means. He just crossed my mind because he was still in my house.

The officers pushed up closer to me and shifted around to protect the paramedics next to me. My racing heart was beginning to slow and become more methodical. A better, less panicked rhythm. This horror was almost over.

***

The wailing of the siren faded as the ambulance carrying Connor sped away. I didn't know if he was dead or alive, and I didn't care.

All the adrenaline that was coursing through my veins subsided, and my knee hurt something awful. Immense throbbing took over from toes to hip. I rolled onto my side to take the pressure off. Ol' youngster cop told me to roll onto my stomach. Once I complied, three other officers moved in and cuffed my hands behind my back.

"What's going on here? This is my house. That guy you just took away is one of the suspects. The other is sprawled out on our bedroom floor with half a pecker. These cuffs aren't necessary." Given my age vs. Connor's, I was confused as to how they could mistake me for an intruder.

No one answered my question. Or responded to me at all, until another cop walked up. I raised my chin from the concrete and recognized the face immediately. Officer William "Willy" McCann. Back in the day, Officer McCann was one of my young snot-nosed trainees at Boston PD. Only now he wasn't just an officer, and this wasn't Boston. Chevron stripes were displayed upon both sleeves of his uniform. It was Sergeant McCann now, and this was Nashua PD.

"Holy shit, *Sergeant* now, huh. And you left Boston for Nashua? Ain't that some shit. Nice work, Willy. Now, can you tell these boys who I am and get these cuffs off me? There's another thug in my house, and I want to see my wife."

"It's been a long time, Detective Bishop. I can't exactly do that for you right now."

"It's Detective Bishop now? What's with the formalities, Willy? Cheryl and I are victims here. You have no idea what we've had to endure all night.

Where is she? I want to see her."

Willy didn't respond to me. He ignored everything I'd just said and looked at his officers. "Officer Clark, call an ambulance for the former detective here. That kneecap looks like it's about to fall off. And I'm fairly sure his nose used to be at the center of his face."

The young man simply followed his orders. "Sir, yes, sir."

"The rest of you guys get him up and put him in the back of my car until the ambulance gets here. We need to get inside and check on this other suspect."

The guys picked me up and I put all my weight on my strong side. Young and strong, they practically carried me to Willy's car. After putting me in the backseat, they shut the door and gathered behind one of the cruisers closer to our house. Coming up with a plan for how to enter, I was guessing. Willy knew the layout of my house. He and his wife, Misty, used to come over for BBQs after Willy passed training. Once I left patrol and was promoted to detective, I rarely saw him much.

These guys had to think tactically. Sure, I'd told them Jason was in the bedroom, but so much time had passed he could have been anywhere in there. All they knew was that he was still inside. None of the units on the perimeter called out that he'd escaped. I would have heard it on their radios.

Just a few minutes after their tactical briefing plan, all of Nashua's finest went running into my house with guns drawn. All except Willy, of course. A man with his rank doesn't put himself in the direct line of danger anymore. That's not saying anything bad about him, it's just the nature of the position.

I looked around, and for the first time since coming outside, I noticed every neighbor in the area was crowded around. All of them pressed up as close as they were allowed against the yellow caution tape. I couldn't make out faces because most had cell phones in front of them. It was the age of the cell phone, after all. And many new young couples lived in the neighborhood—I bet some of these people already had a thousand *likes* on the videos they'd been sharing to their Facebooks, Twitters, Vines, and Snap … whatever's. That was real life to them. This house-of-horrors story would mean nothing to them. Only the amount of attention they'd get from recording it would. Our well-being wasn't their first concern, and that was disheartening. The ones without phones in front of their faces—people our age—looked terrified. Terror in our quiet town was unheard of.

I wondered how Cheryl was doing. She must have been going crazy not knowing what happened to me. I needed to let her know I made it out.

"Hey Willy, can you let me call the hospital where Cheryl is? I need to let her know I'm okay. And you can take these cuffs off now, this is a little overkill for a victim," I called out of the iron-bar-covered window.

His lack of response brought on a surge of uncertainty.

What the heck is going on?

"Will—what the hell, man?"

Willy's lips pursed and he dropped his head. After

pondering his thoughts for a few seconds, he finally walked over to me. The window was down about halfway, and the cool morning air felt exceptional as it wicked away body heat.

"Jerry. I want you to listen to me carefully. You're going to be placed under arrest. So, I—"

"Under arrest? What are you talking about? Willy. These are the guys, or one of them at least, that killed Jenny Wilson! Do you remember that case? I know you do. You must. No one could ever forget that case. And that guy that just left in the ambulance, his name is Connor. And he confessed to the whole thing. Said his girlfriend was in on it too."

Before Willy could say anything, I heard yelling from my house as the officers cleared each room.

"Nashua Police. If anyone is in here, come out with your hands up!"

"Shit, the media are starting to arrive," Willy said, drawing my attention to the incoming road behind me. "Jerry, listen. You just shot a man. No doubt in self-defense, but you know it's procedure to conduct an investigation on that, along with all that went on here." I can't imagine what you and Cheryl have been through, but I still have to do my job right. Everyone involved deserves that transparency."

"Willy, listen. They raped Cheryl. Forced her to do things. The guy in the ambulance was about to knock her teeth out one by one with a punch and hammer!"

The color dropped from his face and he scratched at his freshly shaven jaw. "Shit man, I'm so sorry. You know I love Cheryl, and I want these guys punished for what they've done. But I have to go by the book. And the first thing you need, Jerry, is a doctor."

"Get this done and take me to Cheryl! I'm refusing all medical treatment until I see my wife. So do what you have to do for your investigation, and do it fast."

As the news vans raced in, Willy started to walk back toward his men. I called out for him to come back. This might be the last time I got to talk to him without a lawyer and audio recordings.

"Willy, do me a favor—find a girl named Vanessa who went to high school with Jenny Wilson. Check the past students list and the list of those who got expelled during that time. She helped Connor kill and rape that poor girl. You won't have much time. Once she realizes Connor isn't coming home, she's going to disappear. You have to find her."

He turned back to me. "Since I'm with Nashua PD now, I no longer have access to Boston PD files. But I still have some buddies there that can probably look into it. I'll see what I can do."

"Thanks, Willy. Now I'm begging you—take me to see Cheryl."

News anchors and cameramen popped out of their perspective vans and yelled questions all at the same time. Willy disregarded them the same way he had initially done to me. He was focused on my front door.

Moments later, I saw four officers carrying Jason out like he was their brother who had just been wounded in combat. I hoped they didn't feel that way about him. I hoped they were just doing their jobs without that emotion. I also understood that they had to see Jason as a human. For now.

The monster was barely conscious, that much I could tell. I didn't know Connor's condition, but it hadn't looked good for him—I'd hit my mark. But if he lived, he would never admit to the police what he'd done to Jenny. He would say I made it all up. Maybe we could turn Jason against him. After all, he left him there to die or get caught.

There was only one thing to do—I had to find Vanessa.

14

DUE TO MY CONDITION, I was transported to the hospital instead of jail, where I refused all treatment until I was permitted to see Cheryl. It wasn't an unrealistic demand, but with the demand came the consequence of being denied pain medication. The pain in my knee was making me nauseous now. And having one arm handcuffed to the bed rail just further added to my anger. Even with these current circumstances, I was able to smile as soon as Cheryl walked in.

"Oh my god, Jerry!" Cheryl said as she entered my room past the guard at the door. She was wearing men's sweatpants and an oversized hooded sweatshirt that read *Gate City: Nashua, NH* in yellow writing across the front. She must have caught me reading it. "It was slim pickings for clothing in the hospital's lost-and-found box." She laughed.

It was good to hear that laugh again.

She kissed my forehead while making sure not to touch my battered nose. Surveying me and my damage, she said, "We're battered, but we're alive. We made it honey." Her voice quivered.

"We sure did." I pulled her hand close for a kiss.

"Oh Jerry, I was so scared you weren't going to make it out of there. Connor had gotten his hands free and I—" Cheryl was sobbing into the crook of my neck. "I felt horrible for leaving you there. I ran as fast as I could to the guard stand. I figured the guard could radio for police while coming back to the house with his gun. Turns out, our guards don't carry guns, only pepper spray. He called the police as soon as he saw the looks of me, but he refused to go to the house. Said police were better equipped for these situations. I couldn't believe it. I tried to get back to you, but he kept me in the guard stand. I'm so sorry I left you." She was crying so hard her body was convulsing. Snot and drool poured from her face down to my collarbone.

"Shh, it's okay. You did exactly what you should have done. What I needed you to do. And sticking that punch in his leg was a good move!" I needed her to know it and believe it. "You were very brave and never stopped. You're my hero, Cheryl." I meant every word.

We sat and held each other and cried together for the better part of five minutes, each of us silent in words but heavy in thought. I stayed in the moment, squeezing my wife in my arms and thanking God that I got the chance to feel her warmth again.

After taking some time to compose ourselves, Cheryl broke the silence.

"Jerry, what happened after I left? Why were you arrested? I'm not understanding any of this," she said, pointing to the uniformed officer at the door.

I explained to her about shooting Connor in the back and how it looked bad because he was unarmed at that moment. I also told her I wasn't worried about it. That was true. He could have been running after her, knowing she wasn't able to move that fast. And he still had the knife in his pocket. I had no doubt he would have used it if he caught up to her. I'd had to protect her. Willy was simply going by the book, just as he said. But my arrest wasn't my primary concern. With Cheryl safe, my focus was on Connor.

Just who was Connor? I pondered that. I knew who he said he was. I knew who I saw him to be. But who was he *really?* I had only recently re-opened Jenny's case. How was he able to get wind of it? I hadn't made any news appearances that time around. There were no flyers or tip lines. No more grieving parents on television. It was like he heard my thoughts, then showed up at my door. Unless someone from Boston PD tipped him off when I put in the electronic request for the case file—but I felt like I was reaching. No one at the PD would have known who Connor was. But I had to think differently this time around. And that meant considering even the crazy possibilities.

For years, this mystery man had evaded me and a team of highly trained detectives. Eluded all nearby surveillance footage. Escaped justice and gotten away with rape and murder. And I was supposed to believe the thing that spooked him was an old, washed-up private investigator with minimal resources? There had to be more to it.

One thing I did believe was that Jason wasn't involved in Jenny's untimely and gruesome ending. He was a young thug who willingly hopped on Connor's coattails and rode them to my front door. And he paid the price for it.

There was more to Connor and his story. And I intended on getting to the bottom of it. This time, there would be no quitting.

"Cheryl, you have to listen to me carefully. I need you to help me find Vanessa. Call Seamus and see how much he can dig into the old files, then go to my office and see if her name is listed anywhere on my computer case files."

"I'll do whatever you need, but only on one condition—you agree to medical treatment now. The doctors say the way your knee is situated, it could be cutting off circulation to your foot. You need to get this taken care of right away."

I agreed with my wife. She was always putting me first, and she had a valid point. Plus, I wouldn't be able to do any kind of work in this condition.

Feeling satisfied for the moment, I agreed to see the orthopedic surgeon, Dr. Dewanje.

After numerous X-rays and an MRI, Dr. Dewanje determined I needed to be admitted to the hospital and have my knee replaced immediately. The doctor explained that given the way my knee was dislocated, along with all the movement and walking I had done, there was significant damage to the joint, ligaments, and surrounding tissue. A knee replacement was my only option.

The surgery was scheduled for the following morning. I thanked the doctor for his care as he left the room.

A short time later, Willy knocked on the open door and asked if he was interrupting.

"Not at all, Sergeant. Come on in."

"Okay, Jerry. We can stop with the formalities now. I had to do that so my men wouldn't think you were getting any sort of special treatment. I hated having to do that to you, but at the time it was for your best interest. You have to know that."

"I understand, Willy. I'm just bustin' your balls. What's up?"

"Connor is still alive. He had surgery for a shot to the lung, but other than that, damage was minimal. You had regular ball ammunition in that old duty weapon of yours, huh?"

"Yeah, they took the hollow-point bullets when I retired. Fortunately for me … or should I say him, since hollow points would have torn some things up in there. The outcome would have been very different."

"Agreed. I have to tell you both, Connor and Jason are both in this hospital. Standard operating procedure would have been to take victims and suspects to different hospitals, but with the severity of all injuries, we had to go with the closest."

Cheryl didn't like this at all. "So, you're saying those guys who tortured us all night are right down the hall? That I walked past their rooms on the way here?" She sounded terrified.

"Unfortunately, yes. Connor is in the ICU and will be here in recovery for at least a couple weeks. But Jason ... there wasn't much they could do for his penis. The nub he's left with for life is all he gets."

"Ha." Cheryl exclaimed, followed by an uneasy laugh.

I looked at Cheryl with a broken heart. Raising our interlaced fingers to my lips, I kissed the top of her hand.

"Good job on defending yourself with that one, Cheryl," Willy chimed in. "Jason will be transported to county jail tomorrow."

"I'm honestly glad both boys will survive. If only to face their punishment. Death would have been too easy on them." Cheryl said exactly what I was thinking. I squeezed her hand in agreement.

Just then, a nurse in pink scrubs entered the room. *Sarah R.* was displayed on her name tag, with a sticker of a yellow smiley face next to it. "Hello all, I'm Nurse Sarah from the Psychiatry Department. I'm here to take Cheryl for her appointment on the first floor."

"I don't want to leave my husband. Can I reschedule?"

Before Sarah could reply, Jerry interjected. "Go ahead, honey. The faster you begin treatment for a traumatic event, the better chance of getting a hold on PTSD before it gets outta control."

"Your husband is right. It's only an hour long and I will bring you right back, I promise."

Cheryl looked at me and Willy, then nodded slowly.

"Honey," I said, "I know you're scared; I am too. But you are the strongest person I know. It's one of the reasons I fell in love with you. We will get through this together and come out stronger than ever. But we won't be able to do it alone. We both need to accept the help so we can recover faster." It destroyed me inside to see her that way. I still had an obligation to make sure my wife was taken care of, and ensuring her mental health was part of it.

"Okay. I won't be gone long." Cheryl started toward the door. "Oh and Willy, you keep an eye on him while I'm gone, you hear."

"Yes ma'am, you got it."

15

As soon as Cheryl was gone, I took the opportunity to speak to Willy freely.

"Willy, I need a favor. I need to you to get me in the room with Jason."

"Are you crazy? For what purpose?"

"I need to see if he'll give me information on Vanessa. A last name. Where she lives. Something. I would ask you to do it, but if he invokes his Miranda rights, you won't be able to talk to him at all. I'm just a citizen now; his right to remain silent doesn't apply to me."

Willy's hesitation showed concern at my request, but also showed he didn't want to say no. He was torn between legality and the overall benefit.

"I need it to happen today. My surgery is tomorrow and by the time I come out of it and sober up from the anesthesia, Jason will already be at County. By that time, it will be too late."

"How will you get past the guard at Jason's door? He's a young cop, but not stupid."

"Shit." I hadn't thought about another guard.
"Any ideas?"

Willy pulled keys from his pocket and released
my handcuffs. "He's in Room 504, down the hall to
the left. Shift change is in thirty minutes; the staff
will all be surrounding the computers at the nursing
station at that time. I will take both officers to the
doctor's conference room to discuss upcoming
transports or something. You will only have about
a five-minute window before the oncoming nurses
make their rounds. And with that knee, that doesn't
seem like very much time."

"That's plenty of time. You haven't seen what I've
been capable of on this knee." I threw Willy a wink.

"Yeah, yeah, Mr. Tough Guy. Five minutes. Your
time will start when I walk away with your guard.
Don't make me regret this, Jerry."

"I'm old and rusty, but my detective skills never
fade. I won't let you down."

***

Just like clockwork, Willy walked away with my
guard exactly thirty minutes later. I waited a few
seconds as all the nurses walked together past my
room to begin their briefings. I grabbed the crutches
left beside my bed that were meant to help me get to
the bathroom and hobbled as fast as I could down the
hall. When I got to Room 504, the curtain was pulled
closed..

My eagerness to get to Jason caused a flutter in my

stomach. An expanding feeling in my chest by hyper-
alertness drove me to move on. I pulled open the
curtain, hopped into the room, and closed the curtain
behind me. *Here lies the man who raped my beloved wife.*
I begrudgingly had to dismiss the revolting thought
as fast as it came. I wasn't here about that now.

Jason rolled over from facing the window and
looked annoyed, as if he'd expected just another
doctor or nurse. When he caught my eye, I saw terror
in his gaze. He reached out to press his nurse call
button. I yanked the cord, causing the button box to
fall to the floor.

"Look man," he replied, "it was all Connor's idea.
He told you that. I didn't know he had your house
picked out for his own reasons. He should be the one
you're after, here. Not me."

My face grew hot with anger at his plea toward
innocence. "Connor may have brought you to my
house, but you made your own choices while you
were there. You raped my wife, you sick fuck. But you
won't be raping anyone now, will you." I snickered
while pointing at the bandages covering the space
where his manhood used to be.

Five minutes.

"You'll have to live with that choice, and the
courts will deal with you later. That's not why I'm
here." I moved in close and softened my tone. Like
the saying goes, you catch more flies with honey
than you do with vinegar. "Listen Jason, I get Connor
dragged you into his mess. He brought you into his
agenda then left you behind to get caught—or killed."
Jason's face dropped. I could see he had already come

to that realization on his own. "I need your help."

"My help?" He was genuinely confused.

"I'm a former cop, as you learned last night. You aren't the one I'm after, Connor is. He raped and murdered a young girl and caused hurt to a lot of people." Catching flies with honey. "I need to know Vanessa's last name, or where I can find her. My guess is she doesn't still live near the high school after all these years. Do she and Connor have a house or apartment together in Boston?

"I don't know man. You met Connor; he will come back and kill me if I tell you that. He cares more about that chick than he does his kid."

"I get that. And he clearly cares about her more than you. Look, what he did to you? He lured you to my house under false pretenses, he ordered you around, then he left you behind to be caught. Think about that. He left you there. On purpose. As he ran to save his own ass." I told him what I thought he'd want to hear. Then I paused. When he didn't reply, I told him, "Just look at it as giving me the address of the *friend* who betrayed you."

Jason looked around the room, while his mouth opened and closed without speaking. He clearly wanted to say something but couldn't bring himself to let it out.

"Look, I know you want to do the right thing now. Connor is the reason you'll never be able to jerk off or have sex with a woman again. If he never brought you to my house, you'd still have a dick. How can you feel like a man without a dick? *He* did this to you." I hoped this was working.

146

With his hand clenched in a fist, he started punching himself in the head. He was realizing all the loss that comes with losing your dick.

"I don't have much time here. I'm not a cop anymore, so nothing you tell me gets used in court. As a matter of fact, I'll tell the cops working your case—guys that are my friends—that you helped me here. That will benefit you when your case goes to court."

His thinking was taking way too long. I could hear movement in the hallways; my five minutes was up.

"Just a name then. Or what she looks like. Anything, Jason. Anything you can give me will help me—and will help you."

"Hey! No one is supposed to be in here." Jason's new nurse grabbed me by the arm.

"I'm sorry, I'm a friend. I just wanted to check on him," I lied.

"This man is a prisoner; he is not allowed visitors."

I stood and lingered to reach for my crutches. I was trying to buy Jason some time. The nurse still had a grip on my bicep and was pulling me toward the door.

"Please, Jason. Think of the little girl. Forget about us and forget about last night. The girl is what I care about." I was actually begging this piece of shit.

I was ushered into the hall by the nurse. Just before I shuffled away, Jason yelled from behind his curtain, "Santana. Vanessa Santana. She's Hispanic but has the brightest green eyes you ever saw. Like those brochures you see of oceans in other countries. That kind of green. That's all I know."

The nurse stood close behind to make sure I didn't go back to Jason's room. She didn't know I'd already got what I needed.

16

AFTER CHERYL WAS OFFICIALLY DISCHARGED as a patient, she eased over into her role as visitor. "Did you have a good visit with the therapist, my love?" I asked as she sat at my bedside.

Her answer hurt my heart. "It was a good discussion. I talked about my most recent fears, which involved having to give the hospital gown back. I didn't know they planned to give me clothes, and all I could think of was having to go home in the cut-open nightgown I arrived in. I didn't want to see that nightgown ever again. Soiled in my vomit and urine. I cried at the thought of it. But when the nurse saw the anguish on my face, she clarified that I would keep the lost-and-found clothes I had on. I told the hospital to burn that gown."

The trauma for us was going to be extensive, beyond what I imagined. I felt like a failure as a protector and as a husband. There was no response I could give that would ease her pain. I simply told her I loved her.

With all my years working violent crimes, I'd

learned to compartmentalize the emotional pain that came with the job. But that pain was because of the empathy I had for the families. It hadn't been my own despair. This torment and anguish had landed at my doorstep. And Cheryl—she'd never had to experience or witness the horrors of this life, until now. I had to address it.

"Honey, listen. It's going to be a long road for us. As much as I want to say those bastards are out of our lives now—they're not. They are going to be in our thoughts and in our nightmares for a while. And saying that pisses me off is an understatement. But we are going to go through it together. Over time, with the help of all these shrinks they're sending us to, we will come out on top. Okay?"

Her head fell forward with her chin meeting her chest. A single tear rolled down her cheek. She took a second for herself. After a deep breath, she raised her head and looked me straight in the eye. "I trust you, Jerry. I'll do whatever you think is best, as long as we're doing it together. We will take it one moment, one hour, then one day at a time. We already know we're survivors. Together forever."

Together forever. That was how we ended our wedding vows. That took the breath right outta me. I leaned in and kissed the tip of her nose. She always loved that.

We had a moment of silence before Cheryl spoke again. "Should we call the kids?"

After discussing it, we decided we weren't ready to call them yet. We weren't ready to relive all the details of the night or for them to see us like this. So, for the rest of the night, we didn't talk. There was no need for that right now.

***

At five o'clock the next morning, the door opened and startled me. I must have dozed off for a bit. Cheryl was asleep, outstretched in the recliner next to me. Once I was satisfied that we were safe, I focused on the door. It was Willy.

"Why are you creeping up on us at O'dark-thirty, Willy?" I whispered so as to not wake Cheryl.

"Sorry, I didn't mean to scare you. I wanted to come talk to you before they took you in for surgery. I have good news, and bad news—which do you want first?"

"Don't play with me, man. Tell me all of it." I was anxious and annoyed.

"Good news is, you're no longer a prisoner. Doesn't mean you're free of any charges down the road, but after forensics and detectives processed the crime scene, meaning your house—all accounts show self-defense and support your fears regarding Connor getting away. I mean, shit, a murdered little dog and *Shadow Was Here,* smeared on the wall? That's some of the sickest shit I've ever seen. The higher-ups agree with me, you shouldn't be in police custody right now," he explained while removing the handcuffs.

"That's great news. Thank you. What's the bad news?"

"Jason wants to file a formal complaint against

you for harassment. He has a nurse as a witness. When the nurse learned you're not actually his friend, she backed him up. We have to take a report, but we will take our time on it. That's about all I can do."

"Pfft. Fuck that guy." My voice was loud and woke Cheryl.

"What guy? Oh hi, Willy, everything okay?"

"Just catching Jerry up on some details before his surgery. Everything is fine."

"Willy is being modest. He has great news. I'm no longer being held against my will. I'm a free man." I told her the parts I thought she should hear as of now.

"That's great news! Thank you for coming to tell us in person."

"I have some information for you too, Will—and I guess this will be news to you too, Cheryl. But don't be mad." Cheryl was about to learn about my hospital encounter with Jason. But not the part about the complaint. "Jason gave me a name. Vanessa Santana. We need to find her fast, before she's spooked by Connor's arrest. I don't know if she lives local and caught the whole ordeal on the news, so we should assume she knows. But I figure it will take her some time to pack up and go, having a baby and all."

"Okay, I'll have my best men on it. If we can get to her, she may crack and give up info on Jenny's murder. I'm pretty confident she will put it all on Connor and probably won't even put herself at the scene. But even that would be great for us right now since Connor is already in custody. I'll get a move on it. Good luck in surgery—or break a leg. Ha, I don't know. Hope it goes well. Call me when you're feeling up to it. Oh, and before I forget, a detective from Nashua PD will be coming by to take each of your statements later today." Willy was off to start the hunt for Vanessa.

"Jerry, my dear. Just how did you get this information from Jason? Obviously, the police didn't give it to you, because you just gave it to them." Busted.

After explaining how I'd gotten into Jason's room, and how I'd gotten the information from him, Cheryl was more proud of me than she was mad. She knew how important finding Vanessa was and how time was of the essence. If Vanessa crossed state lines, she was going to be a lot more difficult to find. In Massachusetts we knew what our resources were, who our confidential informants were … there was a lot of red tape in working with out-of-state agencies.

17

I AWOKE TO BRIGHT LIGHT. My mind was foggy and slow to process my surroundings. *Beep, beep, beep.* A low and steady sound from nearby. Faint voices in the distance. Too far to make out what was being said. I was in the hospital. Now I remembered. I felt drunk. No, more like the stage between when drunkenness fades and the hangover begins.

"Jerry, honey. I'm right here. Your surgery was a success, and doctors say the tissue damage will heal with the help of physical therapy."

I didn't realize Cheryl was sitting next to me. It was like when you're drunk at the wrong time and trying really hard to be sober. I tried to speak but my mouth was too dry, and my lips were stuck together. I pointed to the tray table.

"Water?"

I nodded fast, as if begging without words.

"Here you go." Cheryl handed me the clear plastic cup full of the wonderful wetness I needed.

After gulping two more of those down, my mind wasn't so hazy anymore.

"Much better. Thank you, babe. I heard what you said about the surgery—that's good news."

"I'm happy to hear it was a success," a man interrupted.

I looked up and saw a police officer I had never seen before. A lot of police had been in and out since we got here, but this man was unfamiliar.

"I'm Lieutenant Walker with the Nashua Police Department. I'm so sorry for the ordeal the two of you have been through. I wanted to come by and let you know that I will personally be overseeing the investigation of your case. Crimes like these have never happened in Nashua before. I can't even begin to imagine what you're dealing with, and I won't pretend to. But what I can do is have all my best officers and detectives working around the clock to sort this all out and get justice for you."

He paused, but we didn't interject.

"The lead detective is already standing by. Detective Presidio, will you come in, please?"

I looked towards the open door. A few nurses hurried past, then a doctor with a concerned look on his face carrying a clipboard. Finally, a young man in a well-tailored navy-blue suit emerged from around the corner. He gave a quick wave and nod of his head as he walked in.

"Hello. I'm Detective Presidio, as the boss man here said, but you can call me Stan. I know you have answered a ton of questions already, and you may be asked some of the same questions again, but it's all necessary to build a solid case."

Stan was tall. Six-two probably. His full head of jet-black hair was neatly parted and combed to the side. He had a good barber, indeed. His smooth-shaven face and slight wrinkles at the corners of his eyes led me to believe he was in his mid to late thirties. He carried himself with confidence. I liked him already.

"Pleasure to meet you both. Not sure if you're aware I'm a retired Boston detective and an old buddy to Sergeant McCann."

"Yes, yes. I'm sorry. I'm not meaning to treat you as if you don't know how processes work. I just know it may be different for you being a victim in all of this," Lieutenant Walker replied to my unintentionally condescending comment.

He wasn't wrong. It was different being a victim. I tried to pretend that it wasn't, but I couldn't keep that charade up.

"Yes, it is. It's a very different type of animal being on this side of things. We appreciate all that you and the department have been doing."

"You're welcome. I'll leave you here with Stan. You're in good hands. I'm going to head back to the station. It's important that you try to remember as much detail as possible," the lieutenant said before leaving.

As if we were going to forget any of this anytime soon.

Presidio sat with us for over an hour as Cheryl and I spoke about the terror of the night. Every single horrid detail. We spoke of our fears, as well as our actions—and theirs. Cheryl spoke of the forced oral copulation and sexual assault by Jason. We didn't leave anything out. I let him know of my history with the Jenny Wilson case and all of Connor's admissions. We took breaks to cry, hug, and gather ourselves as we had to relive it all. I felt as if I were telling this man something out of a movie. But it was all too real. Presidio just listened, only asking pertinent questions when they were warranted. He was good at his job; I could tell that much. I know the eagerness he felt wanting us to get to the parts that mattered most. But allowing us, as victims, to tell it as we needed to, as we recalled it, was important. It was necessary.

"Let's just say I wouldn't have any teeth left if Jerry didn't free himself when he did," Cheryl said at the end.

A quiet fell over the room as we all thought of that realization.

"I'm so sorry for what you've been through." It was all he could say. All anyone could have said.

He informed us that once Jason and Connor were medically cleared for incarceration, they would be transferred to county jail, where they would be held without bail. He explained that they already had a hefty list of felony charges pending for both of them. These things were explained in detail more for Cheryl's knowledge than mine.

"We have a ton of physical evidence. It will take our lab several weeks to process all of it, and the DNA collected from your house, but the evidence is there. These guys won't be getting out; that is my personal promise to you both."

Cheryl was biting her bottom lip and picking at her fingernails.

"What is it, Cheryl? I see that look on your face."

She hesitated a good few seconds before unleashing the harsh truth. "I don't know much about the law, but sir, you're saying you can promise that those guys won't get out. I'm sorry, but Jerry made a promise to the Wilsons, and it didn't pan out." She looked down in shame at her thought.

That stung. I wanted to be mad, but I realized I only felt that way because she was right.

Walker didn't know the details of my promise to the Wilsons, but could tell by our demeanor that it was a touchy subject. "Ma'am, I can say with full confidence that they will not be getting released from jail. And if for some god-awful reason, they were to be let out, I would notify you both before that happened."

I patted Cheryl's hand so she would know I wasn't upset with her.

"One last thing—your dog was picked up by animal control. They are aware of the circumstances and will hold Shadow until one of you can contact them with your wishes for her remains. There's no rush. Also, we are done processing your home. You may return at any time."

Cheryl buried her face in my arm and sobbed. My heart was broken and angry. How were we ever going to go back there? I guess in order to be survivors, we had to try and survive.

The detective pulled his business card from his

inside pocket and placed it on my bedside table. "My desk and cell numbers are on there. Call day or night with any questions."

I thanked him for stopping by.

After Presidio left the room, I thought more about what was to come. The horror wasn't over yet but I wasn't about to relay that fact to Cheryl. She believed once Jason and Connor were arrested that it might be cased closed. That was the farthest from the truth.

18

I SPENT THREE DAYS AT THE HOSPITAL after my surgery, then was told it was time to be discharged. Due to the nature of what had happened, they allowed Cheryl to stay with me all that time.

"I've been thinking, Jerry—it's time for us to go home."

"Are you sure?" Honestly, I wasn't even sure.

Connor was still in the hospital recovering, and Jason was locked up downtown. So that brought some sort of relief.

I told Cheryl we could stay in a hotel for a while if that would make her more comfortable.

"We would still need to go home to get clothes and toiletries. Plus, we would just be spending money to delay the inevitable."

She was right. If we were going to have to endure a trial and all that came with it, we needed to take the first step at being strong; going home was that step. It was time, and it needed to happen.

I staggered myself to the bathroom to lose the

hospital gown and put clothes on. I too was given sweatpants, but instead of a touristy Nashua shirt, the nurse gave me a Disneyland t-shirt with Mickey and Minnie largely displayed on the front. "I've never even been to Disneyland," I told her. She said it was the only thing left in the lost-and-found box. How embarrassing.

When I emerged from the bathroom wearing my poser shirt, Cheryl started cracking up. Laughing so hard tears rolled down her cheeks. I would take embarrassment to hear her laugh like that any time. Tragedy allows you to appreciate the small things.

***

When we got inside the house, we both stopped in the entryway, looking around and listening to the silence. No more commotion here. The light from the bedroom had been left on and illuminated the landing upstairs. I stepped over the spot of blood where Shadow lost her life and led Cheryl around it. I looked at her face to see how she was doing. I knew that if I asked, she would say she was fine, even if she wasn't.

Her eyes were bulging and her grip on my arm was stiff. She was turning white and her hands felt clammy. She was going into shock. "Cheryl, look at me, baby." I lifted her chin so her eyes would meet mine. She blinked a few times and shook her head in denial, like she was having a hard time grasping what had happened here. Shit, I felt the same way. "Let's move from this spot, okay?"

Her posture crumpled, and she covered her mouth with her free hand. Her other hand still had a good grip on my arm. The rosy cheeks she normally displayed were returning. She side-stepped around Shadow's last place and we climbed the stairs together.

The bedroom light provided just enough brightness to guide us down the hall. Cheryl didn't try to avoid the loose boards this time; the creaking sound wasn't going to bother anyone now, and we didn't have to worry about giving away my location.

When we got to our room, neither of us was prepared for what we saw. I was so caught off guard I shoved Cheryl back into the hallway. She wasn't having it and squeezed past me.

Blood. And a lot of it. The red was so dark in color it almost appeared black. Most had been absorbed into the carpet, but the pools that remained on top were coagulated. There were several of these spots, in various sizes. I could almost re-create where I had been when each spot was created. The largest puddle was from my broken nose.

The closet doors still hung from their hinges, but the slats were no longer whole. Small pieces of fractured wood from their destruction were all over the place. "I don't remember seeing those pieces when I spent all that time afraid to look up, or when I was in search of a focal point," Cheryl said softly.

The brain works in funny ways during a traumatic event.

Since our bedroom wasn't large, I didn't need to move far before coming to a vomit stain. It was completely dry by this point. I couldn't smell it anymore, but the stench of urine and the metallic smell of blood filled the room. I'd seen many scenes like this throughout my career, but never in my own home. I became angry and filled with hate. Unlike me, Cheryl wasn't angry—she was devastated.

The foot post of the bed still had 550 cord attached to it. The frayed ends and the way the cord wore the paint from the wood were a reminder of the struggle I put up while being held there. The indents in the wood showed how hard I'd been pulling to free myself.

Mental note: Get rid of all 550 cord left in the garage.

Our bed wasn't in total disarray. The blankets were folded over neatly on each side, showing how methodically and without urgency we had gotten out of bed when the doorbell rang.

Shadow's blood was dry and flaky against the yellow egg-shell-colored paint of the wall. If only every wall in the room had that hideous wallpaper, the blood wouldn't have been so obvious.

Jesus. What kind of animals could do this shit?

As I paced around the room, mentally planning my immediate repairs, Cheryl grabbed hold of my arm.

"Honey, are you okay?"

"I feel like the walls are closing in around me. I stood there staring at the wall, thinking of Shadow's bark and how she wasn't there to greet us when we got home. The room is starting to become dark—there's little lights floating around in front of me."

"Sit down, you're about to faint."

"No. I'm never going to be on the floor of this room again. And I'm damn well sure I'm not going to sleep in this room ever again."

I agreed with her. We walked to the doorway and turned around to scan the room one last time. We would have it professionally cleaned, or maybe I would light it on fire—but we wouldn't be back. I said goodbye to the good memories Cheryl and I had made there, and a good-fucking-riddance to the horror the room now signified.

I flipped the light switch off and closed the door. I stood in the darkness of the hallway and leaned my back against the bedroom door. It was the moment I realized how different I felt. Somewhere between being a victim and an old detective. Somehow older, and now angry. I had been trying to suppress the anger I had been feeling since being at the hospital, but after seeing this room, it was overwhelming, and for now, I was embracing the feeling.

We went to survey the rest of the house together, linked arm in arm. When we got to the bathroom door, I reached in and flipped the switch. Items Cheryl had taken out from under the sink sat strategically lined on the counter's edge. She must have been so careful in setting them down. The medicine cabinet was wide open, and most of its contents now filled the sink. Cotton swabs, Tylenol bottles, Band-Aids, expired prescriptions, and everything else most households stored in their bathroom cabinets. I looked at this stuff and remembered how desperately we needed to find a cutting utensil.

"This is where I stood and prayed to God. I asked Him to please lead me to something I could use. When he did, I realized God answered prayers. Ha! What a joke. God does not answer prayers. Finding nail clippers and a file was not a prayer answered. It was coincidence. Those items would have still been there, whether I prayed or not. If God answered prayers—if God was listening during all those times I prayed to keep my family safe and healthy, you wouldn't be crippled and our doorbell would have never rung in the middle of the night. God is either a joke, or nonexistent. And I'm leaning toward the latter." Cheryl was pissed.

I looked at Cheryl with incredible sadness, hearing her feelings toward God. But I didn't say anything. Her feelings were valid.

My anger at seeing the bedroom and Cheryl's questioning of God's existence felt motivating. It was an anger that lit a fire under my ass.

I kicked away the stuff on the floor in contempt for it having to be there in the first place.

We continued our rounds through the house. Leftover meatloaf was covered in gnats on the kitchen counter. The garage floor was full of tools Connor had pulled from the cabinets and decided not to use on us. The only room that appeared untouched was the living room.

We rested and decided the living room would be our temporary living space. Cheryl used the guest bathroom to shower first.

"Feeling clean now?" I ended up regretting asking the question.

"The water felt extra hot and slightly burned on my skin. I needed to feel cleansed, and hot water to boil the touch of those boys away was the way to do it … Instead of my loofah, I used the sponge I typically used to clean the shower. You know the one?"

I knew the question didn't warrant a reply. I let her continue.

"I poured body wash onto the scouring side and scrubbed my entire body. I finally felt in control."

My eyes looked her body over as my ears were trying to comprehend what she was saying. Blood droplets oozed from small scratches all over her arms, legs, and neck. I presumed the rest of her was the same way, but she had a nightgown on. A new nightgown we'd picked up on the way home.

A big smile took over her face, and it scared me. I was hoping this phase was temporary for her. But as a man—a man who didn't get raped—I could not and should not pass judgment on this woman who had. I simply grabbed hold of her and squeezed her with all the love I had.

We lay together on the couch. I closed my eyes and hoped for a nightmare-less sleep.

Hoped. Because prayer was something we would no longer do.

19

ONCE OUR STORY BROKE on the news, our neighbors, whom we had never spoken to prior to the invasion, were lining up at the door to give us baked goods and home-cooked meals. When the first neighbors stopped by, they rang the doorbell. My heart leaped into my throat. Cheryl looked at me with wide eyes and sat paralyzed. I realized our immediate fear was part of the trauma. I got my bearings and answered the door, where I met Bob and Julie. Julie said they lived down the street. She handed me a homemade lasagna and said how sorry they were to hear about our "incident." Once they'd left, I handed the dish to Cheryl. "More comfort food," I told her before grabbing my crutches and hobbling off into the garage.

When I returned with tools in hand, Cheryl gave me a perplexed look.

"Jerry, what in the world are you doing?"

"I'm disabling the fucking doorbell."

Cheryl followed me to the front door and watched as I cut the wires. I mounted the cover plate back to the stucco wall and pushed the button, ensuring it would never ding again. I looked at Cheryl, satisfied with my small accomplishment. "Done."

"That's my man," Cheryl said before kissing my cheek. I didn't think we could bear hearing another doorbell again.

When the neighbor directly next door came over and introduced herself as Debbie, she was forced to knock. Cheryl insisted on answering the door with me this time. Part of her healing process, she said. "Hi Debbie, I'm Jerry and this is my wife Cheryl." Debbie cried and apologized for not hearing or knowing what was going on just yards from her home. She said Lieutenant Walker and some other officers had knocked on her door shortly after the chaos settled and asked if they had seen or heard anything throughout the night.

"I was startled when the police came," Debbie said. "We just don't have police activity in this area, and I thought something bad must've happened to my husband while he was at work. I had no idea the horrible things that occurred in your house. To you … and your husband." She leaned in to give Cheryl a hug. "I was asleep. I didn't hear screaming or anything. I feel so horrible. Like maybe if I heard something, I could have called the police to save you."

She covered her face and cried. Cheryl hugged her back tightly and told her it wasn't her fault. That we were not mad at her and did not blame her for anything.

Then I thought to myself, *I'm over here trying to deal with my own trauma and we're here comforting this woman. This stranger.*

Cheryl released the hug and thanked her for stopping by. Both women wiped tears from their eyes. I was happy when Cheryl told her that we needed some time to process it all and asked her to respect our privacy. She sniffled and pulled a tissue from her pocket to wipe her runny nose. "Oh of course. I'm sorry. I'm so sorry."

I stepped back inside and shut the door. People were exhausting.

Heading back to the living room, I aimed for the comfort of my favorite chair. As soon as my butt hit the cushiony leather, there was a knock on the door. A short, repeated tapping.

Jesus. People just didn't respect boundaries.

Before I could get up, Cheryl came from the kitchen. "I'll get it, honey. Elevate your leg, you need to rest it. It's obviously another neighbor. I'm thankful people care, but this is getting to be too much."

As Cheryl later told me, she abruptly opened the door, ready to teach Debbie about respect. She was caught off guard to see it wasn't Debbie at all. It was another woman, one she had never met. This woman was younger. Late twenties, early thirties, maybe. Annoyed with these unknown neighbors just dropping by, Cheryl told her, "Thank you for checking on us, but I'm asking all the neighbors to please respect our privacy right now." As she started to close the door, she was shocked when the woman caught it with her hand.

"Oh, I'm not a neighbor. I'm an acquaintance

of your husband, Jerry. Gerald, as I call him. And Seamus. He's a close friend of ours."

Gerald was my birth name. The only people who referred to me by it were my mother, and Cheryl when she was really upset.

Cheryl continued, "Uh, I'm sorry, how do you know my husband? Not to be rude, it's just we've never met, and no one calls him that."

"Like I said, just acquaintances from years back. Can I speak to him for just a moment? I won't take up too much of his or your time."

The woman was pretty and unknown to my wife. And she was calling me by a name rarely known to even my close friends. I'd hated the name ever since I was a boy. Even teachers and coaches always called me Jerry.

Cheryl explained she felt a touch of jealously come on. But she didn't want the woman to sense her lack of confidence.

"Sure, just wait here one second. He's on crutches, so it's going to take him a minute. I'll be right back." She left the door open and came into the living room to tell *Gerald* of the woman here to see me.

"I swear honey, she called you Gerald. And that she's a friend of Seamus too," she said as we walked to the front door together. Moving only as fast as my good leg would allow. But when we got there, she was gone.

"That's strange. No one calls me that except you and my mother. What did she look like?"

Cheryl knew I wasn't one to lie, and despite the

obvious suspicions that might have arisen, she didn't really think I'd had an affair with this woman.

"She was a pretty thing. Olive complexion; long, full, dark wavy hair. Like I said, she was very pretty. She had these bright green eyes you wouldn't believe. You know, I think I saw her in the hospital. While I was waiting for you to get out of surgery, she peeked her head in and said she had the wrong room."

"Wait, she had what?"

"I told you, long dark—"

"No, about her eyes," I cut her off.

"They were this bright green. Like the Caribbean ocean. Very unique."

"Fuck! Where did she go?"

"I don't know. I told her to wait here while I went to get you, and you saw, she was gone when we got here. What's going on?"

It felt like time stopped. A cold chill moved through my body and my jaw dropped. I squeezed my eyes shut and was shaking my head in disbelief. I hobbled out onto the porch and looked down the road in each direction. She must have had a car.

Pressing my fist to my mouth, I tried to gather my thoughts. But my mind was racing, and I couldn't put together a sentence. I punched the exterior of the house. And even though I could see blood running down my knuckles, I didn't feel pain.

Cheryl was asking me what was wrong repeatedly. I heard her, but was still trying to grasp it all.

My chest tightened as my heart rate accelerated.

"Jerry, what the hell is going on? You look like you saw a ghost. Who was that woman?"

"Vanessa. That was Vanessa."

Made in the USA
Middletown, DE
24 October 2020